DREAMING OF THE HIGHLAND WOLF

TERRY SPEAR

PUBLISHED BY:

Wilde Ink Publishing

Dreaming of the Highland Wolf

Copyright © 2024 by Terry Spear

Cover Copyright by Terry Spear

Discover more about Terry Spear at:

http://www.terryspear.com/

Print ISBN: 978-1-63311-099-1

Ebook ISBN: 978-1-63311-098-4

SYNOPSIS

Evander Cameron works for the MacNeill wolf pack, taking their Irish wolfhounds to dog show competitions and breeding them, when one of his charges takes off and meets up with his dream dog—a Scottish deerhound. Evander discovers her owner is the kind of wolf he could really fall for.

Alyth MacBain is breeding her Scottish deerhound with a champion when her dog runs off. Now what is she to do? Her puppies might be a mixed breed and the man who owns the stud dog wants one of the puppies for a stud fee!

Who would have ever thought her dog and Evander's—causing all the trouble they have—could bring them together in such a crazy way? Their chemistry is off the charts when it comes to Evander and Alyth's interest in each other.

But now it appears that someone is intent on stealing her dog to sell her and her puppies and Evander and Alyth have to keep that from happening at all costs.

In memory of Rhonda Kirby who loved her authors and reading was her absolute passion. I'm thankful for her friendship over the years.

1

As kennel manager, breeder, show exhibitor and dog trainer of Irish wolfhounds for the MacNeill wolf pack, Evander Cameron had no one to fault but himself when he opened the kennel door early that pretty summer morning and one of the brindle Irish wolfhounds, Dillon, raced out of the kennel and into the inner baily of the MacNeill's Argent Castle. The way the wolfhounds had been barking before that, Evander had realized something had gotten their interest. He should have made sure none of the dogs were running loose inside the kennel first.

No one could stop Dillon, though several other pack members made wild dashes to grab him. But Dillon had raced out of their reach and through the open gate doors of the castle walls before anyone could stop him.

Before any other dogs escaped with Dillon, Evander grabbed a leash, quickly secured the kennel door, and tore off after him. Dillon was normally well-behaved and wouldn't run off like that unless something or someone grabbed his attention. As soon as Evander ran out through the gates of the castle, he knew just what the dog was after. He smelled a dam in heat.

Dogs.

As a gray wolf, Evander was glad he would choose one she-wolf to mate for life, unlike a dog that would take up with *any* female who came into heat. No loyalty whatsoever.

Clouds dotted the blue sky overhead. Verdant green grass, purple heather, white clouds, and trees covered in green leaves reflected beautifully on the still loch making it picture perfect.

"Dillon!" Whoever's female dog it was, they should have kept her under better control. Then he shook his head at himself over that, since he'd definitely lost control of the clan's own dog.

"Dillon, come back here! Heel! I have a treat for you!" Evander knew nothing would convince Dillon he had a better offer for him than what he was searching for now. "*Madra balbh!*" Dumb dog!

Some of the MacNeill men and women who had followed him outside laughed at Evander, including his younger twin sister Lana. Dillon wasn't in any danger, so no one came to help Evander. It was his folly, his mistake to correct.

Evander thought of changing into his wolf. At six-two, Evander was long-legged, and even as a human, he could run fast, but as a wolf, even faster. Still, he hoped he could just call to Dillon, and he would mind him. *Ha!* As if a dog after a dam in heat would think of anything but mating with her.

From the scent she had left all over the place, the female was a Scottish deerhound, similar in appearance to an Irish wolfhound, advertising across the landscape that she was ready and available. Pups from a union between an Irish wolfhound and a Scottish deerhound wouldn't be disastrous since the dogs looked similar, not that he or the MacNeill clan would want to raise a mix of the pups. Duke Dillon was a champion in his own right and bred with females who were at least champion-sired from all over the country, bringing in a nice chunk of money. Giving free breeding rights wasn't in the game plan. And certainly, siring mixed-breed pups wasn't either.

He would never live it down when he returned Dillon to the castle.

Dillon headed straight for the largest loch on the acreage. A small island covered with lavender flowering heather sat in the center, hosting a number of nesting birds—pink-footed geese, whooper swans, tufted ducks, teals, and cormorants. The island was off-limits to wolves and dogs! Damn it! But the object of Dillon's desire was swimming out to the island. And Dillon was swimming right after her.

For a moment, Evander stood on the loch's bank, contemplating what to do. Should he swim after the dogs as a wolf, or swim after them as a human and put Dillon on a leash and make him come home with him? Or just let them have a good time, then wait for them to return to shore on their own? But what if the deerhound went home and Dillon took off after her next? And then there was the issue of them creating havoc for the birds nesting on the island. He knew Dillon wouldn't harm them, but he had no idea about the female.

Unless he leashed Dillon, Evander figured the dog wouldn't come home with him. Evander stripped out of his clothes and with the leash in his teeth, he dove into the water. With powerful strokes, he swam across the cold loch in pursuit of Dillon. So much for feeding and playing with *all* the dogs this morning first thing.

～

ALYTH MACBAIN WAS DRESSED in a white short-sleeved blouse, a MacBain red, green and white tartan mini kilt, and black boots, ready to open her shop, the Scottish Treasures Gift Shop connected to her home in about twenty minutes when she let her blue Scottish deerhound, Duchess Skye, into the yard for one last bathroom break. At the same time, Skye glanced in the direction of the gate that was out of view from where they could see it around the side of the house. Alyth's heart did a dive. Had she closed the gate to the yard last night after hauling in another load of flowers to plant? She was sure she had. Alyth dashed into the yard and saw Skye tearing off for the open gate.

"No, Skye! Come here!" Alyth ran after her, but she couldn't catch up to the long-legged dog. And Skye had other plans in mind. If she hadn't been in heat, she would have minded Alyth.

Alyth ran inside the house, grabbed her car keys, hopped into her car, and tore after her. She rolled down her window, calling after her, "Skye! Treat time!" But Skye was in full heat and no way could Alyth bribe her to come home if Skye could find a hot dog to mate with instead.

It would be Skye's first time to have puppies, and Cal Sutherland was bringing his champion Scottish deerhound, Magnus, to breed with Skye this evening for a second time after Alyth's gift and clothes shop was closed. Cal had agreed to one more breeding after that, to make sure it took. Though after that, if Skye didn't have any puppies, that wasn't his problem.

If some other dog ruined her if the first breeding hadn't taken effect, it would be disastrous. *Losh.* It was all Alyth's fault. She should have ensured the gate was closed before she let Skye out this morning. Though she was so sure she hadn't left it open. She was normally really good about that.

Alyth hadn't realized just how out-of-control her dog could be when it came to being in heat when she was normally obedient. Well, most of the time. Alyth hadn't broken her of the habit of chasing squirrels or birds when she took her on walks, even though she was on leash. Worst of all, Alyth really wanted the money from the pups to help support her gift shop until it became more profitable!

Skye could have between four and fifteen pups and Alyth could sell them for between 800 to 2000 British pounds. Because Skye was double champion-sired since both her mom and dad were champions, and Cal's stud dog was a champion, Alyth could sell the pups for a greater amount, as long as the pups were healthy. His dog was a blue too and had great lines like Skye's and had produced a number of champions, so the stud fee had been 2000 pounds, the cost of a puppy. She wished the stud owner had wanted just a puppy, but he had asked for the cash fee upfront after servicing her dog three times.

Alyth had already found homes for four puppies of the litter at the higher end of the price scale, but of course they would have to look over the puppies and really make a decision then. Since the breeder wanted a stud fee, she was free to find homes for the puppies. Talk about not counting your chickens before they hatched—only this time with regard to puppies.

She drove after Skye, then saw her take off through the forest and lands owned by the MacNeill clan. She took a deep-settling breath, pulled her car off the road, parked, grabbed the leash, and hurried out of the vehicle. She just hoped she could catch Skye before anyone saw Alyth trespassing on their land. Though the MacNeills were wolves like her so maybe they wouldn't be too upset with her.

At least as much as the MacNeills doted on their champion Irish wolfhounds, they shouldn't be running through the land free. Alyth just had to worry about other dogs that might be on the loose out here. She was running as fast as she could, leash in hand, knowing she couldn't make Skye come to her if Alyth had turned into a gray wolf. The only way she could make her mind was on a leash, she hoped. Skye stood at nearly thirty-inches tall, so she could be difficult to handle, if Skye really, really wanted a dog lover. Which she was sure she did.

Alyth ran up a grassy, green hill, and down again, past a

pasture filled with Highland cows and two calves grazing. They all paused to observe her, curious, adorable. If she hadn't been in a rush to track down her wayward dog, she would have stopped and talked to them. Well, and she had to hurry so she could get back to her shop. Tour buses regularly stopped in at her place, though the first one shouldn't arrive until about ten.

The pasture was bordered by a river on one side, the trees across the river reflecting in the nearly mirror like water, and then she ran through the woods, a couple of twigs catching at her hair and pulling it loose from her bun.

Och, where was Skye going? To the castle?

Alyth suddenly heard a ruckus of birds squawking and tweeting their annoyance up ahead, and she thought Skye was chasing them. Her rapid heartbeat skipped a couple of beats when she smelled a male Irish wolfhound in hot pursuit of Skye. Not only that, but a male gray wolf was also.

Her skin felt chilled on the warm, summer day, even though she had been feeling hot from the run. She was hoping beyond hope she wouldn't have to deal with an irate MacNeill. All she wanted was her dog back safe and sound. She was afraid it was too much to hope for that her dog hadn't been serviced by the Irish wolfhound already. If Cal's dog had already impregnated Skye, everything would be fine though.

Alyth burst out of the woods to see an island in the middle of the loch. She thought the island extended closer to the shore here than anywhere else. A man's clothes were lying on the ground, and she saw him swimming after the two dogs paddling out to the island. It was like a race she'd never witnessed before. And she knew she'd lost the race unless the hot Highlander could stop the dogs from breeding in time.

Birds of every kind were having a fit as they flapped at the unwelcome visitors arriving on the island where Skye raced over the grassy knoll to the other side where Alyth couldn't see her.

The birds flew off and she figured they would return once the dogs were gone. The brindle Irish wolfhound, his tongue hanging out and his tail wagging, was in hot pursuit. He was a pretty color with a brown base coat and blacks and dark brown stripes.

It took a little while longer for the naked man to climb out of the cold water. He paused for a second, getting a whiff of the dogs' scents, tall, muscular, dripping with water, his hands pushing through his wet, blond hair, and then he raced up the incline and then over the hill on the other side to reach the dogs.

Now what? If she swam over there, it was about a quarter kilometer across at the narrowest point, she could get a leash on her dog, maybe, if Skye was entertaining the Irish wolfhound and wouldn't run off again. She figured the man wasn't going to put one on her dog, just his own. Unless Skye followed him back across the loch. Maybe she would—adoring her newfound love —the dog, not the man. Ugh.

Alyth saw the man coming over the hill, his dog on a leash, a full-frontal view of one hot Highlander, muscled legs and arms and chest, a nice package too, sexy, even if she was annoyed with him for letting his dog loose. Though she knew that was illogical thinking on her part since *her* dog had been running loose too. And then there was Skye, trotting behind them as if she was on a family outing, panting, looking perfectly happy.

The wolfhound kept glancing back at Skye, as if he wanted another hot encounter, and she was eager to go along with it.

The man laughed as he was talking to his dog out loud, not even noticing Alyth standing on the shore across the loch. With her wolf hearing and the way voices carried across the water, she could hear him say, "Listen, Dillon, she's not your type. Oh, I know you think so, but she's just a Scottish deerhound and you're an Irish wolfhound and you sire some of the best—"

Dillon suddenly looked from the man to the shore across the

loch and wagged his tail vigorously when he saw Alyth standing there, her arms folded across her chest, scowling at them. *All three of them!* Dillon, for possibly getting Skye with puppies, Skye, for running off, and the Highlander for putting her dog breed down.

The man was frowning at her, studying her, but then his mouth hitched up slightly at one corner. He was probably amused at the way she was looking at him so scornfully while he was in such a state of undress.

He tied the leash to Skye's collar so that he could swim across with each dog on either side of him, while he was holding the leash in the middle between them. Good. At least he was a fast thinker. She could just imagine herself trying to keep the big wolfhound from getting to Skye any further. She was certain the dog had already enjoyed his time with her.

The man started swimming across the loch. It didn't seem to bother him, despite how chilly it had to be.

Though as hot as she was after chasing her dog down, she wouldn't have minded slipping off her boots and cooling her feet and damn! She had to open her shop in five minutes.

She got on her cell phone and texted her employee and gray wolf friend: *Nita, go ahead and open the shop without me. I'll be there as soon as I can.*

Nita texted her back: *Opening the shop now.*
Thanks!

Ten minutes later, the man and dogs climbed out of the water onto the shore where she was standing. Both dogs shook off the excess water all over her and the man. Och! She had to work, for heaven's sake!

"Your deerhound?" he asked, still smiling a little, grabbing his boxer briefs off the shore.

"Aye." There was nothing to smile about. At least not for

Alyth. Skye was perfectly happy with her newfound friends, her eyes bright with gaiety.

"I'm Evander Cameron. And you are?" the naked guy asked Alyth, pulling on his boxer briefs.

Totally pissed off!

"I'm Alyth MacBain. And that is Duchess Skye." The hussy, Alyth wanted to say.

"She's a beautiful dog."

Alyth ground her teeth. He didn't think so at all, not from what he was saying to his dog about deerhounds before Alyth caught his eye and he had abruptly shut up.

"This is Duke Dillon," he said.

Despite being amused he was a "duke," while Skye was a "duchess," Alyth pursed her lips. She wanted to scream she was so frustrated. Now what should she do? Continue to have Cal's dog service her two more times and hope that Dillon hadn't impregnated her? That's what she would have to do. Pretend that none of this had happened. Cal wouldn't care if the puppies were mixed or not. His stud dog had already done his deed once, so she was stuck for the stud fee anyway. And he had nothing to do with the puppies after they were born. Except that he could crow about having another batch of puppies, if they were his stud dog's, and especially if any of the puppies became champions in their own right.

"So you're from around here," Evander said.

"Aye. I own a shop about a kilometer and a half from the border of the MacNeill property. I had to drive after Skye, not knowing where she was going, and of course here she is trespassing on the MacNeill lands. I had to park off the road to chase her over the hill, past the Highland cows in their pasture, through the woods, and finally to the loch."

Evander smiled and untied his leash from her dog's pink

rhinestone collar, now sopping wet but held onto the collar so Alyth could attach her own leash.

After Alyth did, she tried to pull her dog away from the male, but Skye wasn't having any of it. Alyth needed to get her to her car and on her way so she could get to work! She hoped at least while Skye was having her little run, she had found the time to fully relieve herself! What a disaster. Between vet bills, the stud fee, and feeding bills for all the pups until they went home to their new owners? She shook her head at herself.

"Let me finish getting dressed and we can drop my dog off at the kennel. Then I'll help you get your dog to wherever you're going," Evander said, slipping his shirt on over his head.

"I can manage, thank you." But as much as Alyth tried to get Skye to mind her, she was of a mind to stay with Dillon. "Maybe if you leave, then she'll go with me."

Evander pulled on his pants. "Aye, we can try that, but Skye seems to have a mind of her own."

Tell Alyth about it! She was feeling aggravated to the hilt and there wasn't anything she could do about it. Evander must have been about six-two, and she was only five-four, so making her dog mind only worked when Skye was eager to please her—not like right now.

He pulled his socks and then his boots on.

"I'm trespassing."

Evander smiled at her and finished tying on his boots. "You had good justification. We don't want people just roaming all over the land for no good reason. But you're a gray wolf like us and not one of the enemy clan members who could be up to mischief. You were just trying to reclaim your deerhound that got away from you, so no problem."

But she was doing business with Cal Sutherland, and *he* was an enemy of the MacNeill clan, she knew for sure. Not that it made any difference to her. She wasn't aligned with any of them. And Cal had beautiful, champion deerhounds. The MacNeills only had the more muscled Irish wolfhounds.

She still thought that she might get Skye under control once Evander's dog was back in his kennel. Then again, she could imagine Skye wanting to join *all* the dogs in there to have some more good, hot, loving fun.

Alyth didn't figure anything would happen when they went to Argent Castle, since she was being escorted there by one of the men who worked for the MacNeills and must be part of the pack. But boy was she wrong. There must have been ten men in the inner bailey, all of whom were sword-fighting with their shirts off, but every one of them stopped what they were doing to turn and look at her walking beside Evander and the two dogs, then smiled.

"Hey, Evander, you found Dillon, we see," one of the men said.

Smiling, Evander waved at them. "After a swim. Aye." To Alyth, he said, "That's Lord Ian MacNeill and his brothers, Duncan, Guthrie, and Cearnach, and a couple of cousins."

Ian, the lord of the castle and the leader of the wolf pack. Great.

Skye was whining and yipping excitedly to get into the kennel with all the hot doggies. They were barking, eager for her to join them.

"Hey, let me give you a lift back to your vehicle," Evander said. "I don't think she's going to leave here willingly."

Alyth sighed. "Yeah, I agree. Thanks, I need to get to my shop." She had to admit Evander was nice and trying to be super helpful, despite that she was feeling so annoyed.

Suddenly a woman came out to greet them before they could get into his car and Evander shook his head. "My sister, Lana."

"Hey, Alyth, I can't believe you came here." Lana petted Skye. "Oh, what a pretty deerhound."

"Skye ran away."

"Naughty dog." Lana looked up at Alyth and smiled. "Do you have the new Cameron mini kilts in yet?"

"You know Alyth?" Evander asked, sounding astonished.

"Yeah, I shop at her gift shop anytime I need something Scottish. She has the cutest things. You know that fuzzy little Highland cow I got for Julia for Christmas? That came from Alyth's shop."

"Thanks," Alyth said. "Aye, the Cameron kilts came in."

"Oh, great. I'll drive her there," Lana said.

Evander gave his sister a look that said he could strangle her. "I'm taking her to her car. Skye isn't eager to leave here."

"Okay, fine, you take her to her car, and I'll run by the shop a little later."

"That sounds like a good plan." Then he had to put Skye in his car because Alyth couldn't budge her from the door to the kennel.

Alyth hoped Nita was doing fine at the shop in the mean-time without her.

"See you later," Lana said.

Alyth smiled. She hoped she had lots of sales to make up for the rest of this disastrous day. "Thanks."

When Evander drove Alyth to her car and parked, she thanked him, and got out. Alyth had every intention of pulling Skye out of the back seat, but she wouldn't move.

"Skye." Alyth was at her wits end. "Come." Her sweet, gentle giant was a monster when in heat.

Evander's car smelled like Dillon and a couple of more male wolfhounds had ridden in the back seat.

"I'll get her. Come on, girl." Evander actually carried Skye out of the car, and once Alyth opened the back door, he put her dog inside, and she hurried to shut the door.

"Thanks. Sorry for all the trouble you went through with having to chase Dillon down, and then having to swim across the loch."

"I made a mistake in opening the kennel door before I knew Dillon was loose in there." He ran his hands through his wet hair and acted like he wanted to ask her something.

But she was late to work. At least her shop was in front of her home so she could let Skye out whenever she needed to relieve herself—as long as the stupid gate was closed.

"Bye," she said.

"Bye."

Then she drove off, still fuming about everything, the dog running off, possibly having *half* Irish wolfhound pups, and being late for work. She handled online orders while Nita handled the store front so she hoped Nita wasn't too busy with both, though she hoped they had lots of business at the same time.

And then she recalled Evander's dripping wet, hot, muscled body and smiled. Well, seeing him had been the best part of the morning so far.

2

E vander knew he would get a ton of ribbing when he returned to the castle. Ian and his brothers were just finishing up sword practice and every one of them joined him at the kennel.

Ian slapped him on the back. "If I hadn't known better, I would say you planned the whole thing."

Guthrie laughed. "We wondered why Dillon had torn off like he had. After a deerhound in heat?" He laughed again.

"Yeah, well you didn't have to swim across the loch to fetch the two of them." Though after meeting the lass and learning she was a wolf too, he would have swum across an ocean to retrieve Dillon and her dog.

"Bird Island?" Ian asked.

"Yep."

"And?" Cearnach asked.

"Well, if her dam wasn't already having pups by some deer-hound, Dillon might be the daddy if she ends up with pups."

Duncan laughed this time. "Fifty-seven to sixty-five days from now you could be getting a vet bill for a bunch of little deerhound-wolfhounds."

"If we proved their parentage. She could have been with any number of other dogs." Evander went into the kennel to exercise the dogs, the castle gates now closed.

He thought the brothers would tend to their own business, but no, they weren't done giving him a hard time. Not that he couldn't handle it, after all the ribbing he'd given the brothers and their cousins over the years.

"How did the deerhound find her way here?" Duncan asked. "Maybe you hadn't planned it, but the lass had."

Evander shook his head. "She looked frazzled from the ordeal, running in designer boots in a mini skirt, her dark brown hair falling from her bun." She was beautiful.

"She did look a wee bit frazzled," Cearnach said, smiling. "Wait. So she saw you swimming in...?"

"The loch."

"Wearing?" Cearnach continued.

Evander let out his breath.

Cearnach laughed. "In the raw."

"Aye, but I didn't see her until I was returning with both the hounds and before I began swimming to shore." Evander probably would have left his boxer briefs on when he went to fetch Dillon and her dog, if he'd known the owner was a female and close by.

"Then you asked her to go out on a date?" Ian asked.

"She was in a rush to get to work and take her dog home. Our dog had just ravished hers and I'm sure she wasn't pleased."

Cearnach scoffed and folded his arms. "You rescued her dog and didn't ask her out? That would have been the perfect timing."

"We could charge a stud fee for the service," Guthrie said, as their financial advisor, though Evander knew he was joking. Well kind of. If Ian had gone along with it, Guthrie would be game.

Ian let out his breath. "If there's one thing we don't have enough of, it's eligible she-wolves to mate. Tell her if her dog ends up pregnant, we'll pay for the vet bill. And ask her out for all the trouble this could cause."

"Or one of Heather's brothers will do it," Cearnach said.

Heather MacNeill MacQuarrie was Ian and his brothers' cousin, and all three of her brothers were bachelors.

"I'll do it," Evander said. "It was my mistake. I'll take care of it." Maybe Alyth was seeing someone already! But he could offer to pay the vet bill and feel the situation out.

Then his sister, Lana, and Heather joined him. "We're going to Alyth's shop. Do you want me to pass along any message?"

Everyone looked at Evander. "Nay." He didn't need his sister getting involved in this. Not when he wished to further apologize and get to know the lass better—if she was feeling the same way about him and she didn't have some other man in her life already.

His sister cocked a brow. "Did you ask her out on a date?"

He frowned at his sister. "She was late for work." And tired out. He wanted to catch her at a better time than that.

"Och, you could have asked her on a date for all the trouble you caused her."

"*Her* dog was running loose!"

"So was ours. I'll tell her you're sorry again." Then Lana and Heather headed out in her car and Evander wished that Lana hadn't already known Alyth.

"So what happened?" Nita Chisolm asked Alyth as soon as she dropped off Skye at her house and entered the shop. Nita's pretty, strawberry blond hair was bound in a bun, and she was wearing one of the long Chisolm kilts they had for sale in the shop.

Alyth always gave Nita the latest tartan fashions in addition to her hourly wage to model them and since the fabric was so expensive, Nita loved the arrangement.

"I forgot to lock the gate and Skye bolted. You wouldn't believe where she got off to."

"With those long legs of hers, anywhere, I imagine." Nita was straightening some of the tartan scarves.

"She made it all the way to Argent Castle."

Nita's blue eyes widened. "No. Oh, she's in heat!" Then she smiled. "Did you meet some of those hunky MacNeills?"

"I didn't actually meet them as speak to them, but Evander Cameron pointed them out to me."

"Cameron? Any relation to Lana Cameron?" Nita asked.

"Lana's brother." Alyth didn't have any plan to tell Nita all the nitty gritty details of how Evander retrieved Skye for her, or that his own dog probably had his way with her. She suspected Dillon had, and she didn't have the courage to ask if Evander had seen them getting it on.

"I haven't met him. Is he single and available?"

"How would I know that?"

"So, he helped rein in Skye?"

"Aye."

"Then you should have asked him out or to come over for a meal to thank him." The phone rang and Nita answered it. "Scottish Treasures Gift Shop. Aye, we have the new mini kilts in. Campbell? Aye. See you soon." When Nita got off the phone, she said, "We made three sales and had four phone orders before you arrived."

"Oh, good."

"So what happened to Skye? Did she get knocked up by another dog?" Nita asked.

Alyth groaned. "Hopefully Cal's dog did the trick beforehand."

"But?"

"Probably Evander's dog got to her too. If Cal's dog came through on the first breeding, that's all that matters."

"Oh, so that's how Evander caught up to her. What a little hussy."

Alyth smiled. "I know. That's exactly what I was thinking."

Nita leaned against the counter. "An Irish wolfhound and a Scottish deerhound?"

"Aye. I don't want to even think about it. It sure wasn't what I planned for. All those mouths to feed, the vet bill, the cost of paying for the stud fee, and who knows if I can sell the pups if they're a mixed breed. On top of that, four people already want four of the pups—pure deerhound pups, not a mixed breed."

"Oh, uhm, that's not good. No more talking about them until you know for sure what they are. It'll all work out somehow. Just don't—quit the day job. I don't blame you for being upset about it though. Oh, look, there's Lana Cameron and Heather MacQuarrie. It appears that you brought some business from Argent Castle with you."

"Lana had asked me if the Cameron mini kilts came in." Alyth got on the computer to order some more items for the store and managed one order before the ladies entered the shop.

"Good." Nita went to the door and opened it. "Good morning, ladies. We got the kilts in."

Alyth left her computer to greet them too.

"Ian and my brothers will have a fit if I wear a mini-kilt," Heather said, "but I'm thrilled to get the MacQuarrie one. My mate will love it." She ran her hand over the tartan fabric. "I'll just try it on to make sure it fits."

"Me too," Lana said. "And if my brother hasn't already asked you out, he will. He's just a little shy."

Alyth didn't think Evander was shy in the least, but he was probably annoyed with her for letting her dog get loose and then he had to chase after his dog because of it. *If* he was even interested in dating her. Which shouldn't have bothered her since Evander didn't *even* think deerhounds were as worthy as wolfhounds. But she couldn't stop thinking about the way he had taken control of her dog and helped her out when Skye wouldn't mind her! Not to mention his naked hot physique kept appearing in her mind's eye when she shouldn't be thinking of that at all! At least she now knew he wasn't mated or dating anyone though.

She was beginning to think that maybe breeding dogs was going to be far more work than it was worth. In Scotland, a dam could only be bred four times in her lifetime, so this first one could be a total bust.

Heather said, "Five other MacNeill ladies, including our pack leader Julia, are coming over to order some mini kilts too. I'm sure there will be some MacQuarries coming too. It helps that I'm mated to Enrick MacQuarrie and so have some ties with their pack members at Farraige Castle also. Even though I visit Argent Castle often, Enrick and I live nearer to my pie shop at our home out there."

Nita glanced at Alyth and smiled.

Alyth felt her heart sing. Maybe her shop would now start to get some real business and she wouldn't have to worry about the money from the sale of the puppies after all. Though she'd been looking forward to having oodles of puppies to play with and show off at the store and advertise too. After all, who wouldn't adore puppies? Maybe she would make a sale or two still. Though now, that was iffy, depending on what breed of pups she ended up with.

Lana picked out a scarf and a Cameron crest pin. "And you know, Julia Wildthorn is becoming more and more famous with her wolf shifter romance books, so once she begins shopping here, you can bet she'll endorse your shop."

"Oh, that gives me an idea," Alyth said, getting excited about the whole prospect. "We can carry her books here because she's a Scottish-American author, writing about Highland were-wolves, married to a Highland lord and living in his castle—"

"Which was at one time *her* castle." Heather smiled.

"Oh, how fascinating. We could have a write-up about her and a book signing when she has new releases out too." Alyth had never considered such a thing before, though she did carry books about Scotland in her shop.

"She would love that." Heather picked up a pill box with a hand-painted thistle on it and set that and her mini kilt on the counter.

Lana brought over several items and the two ladies checked out.

"We'll send more business your way as soon as the other ladies see all the goodies we bought," Lana said.

"Thanks, you don't know how much I appreciate it," Alyth said, beginning to think Skye's morning flight might not have been such a bad thing after all. Maybe she had nothing to worry about where Magnus, the prolific stud dog, was concerned. Magnus meant big, powerhouse, great. Surely, that all meant something. Maybe his first attempt succeeded, and she was all set and Dillon was just a fun excursion. Then again, Dillon meant lion or loyal. Maye *he* was more stud material.

After the ladies finished paying for their purchases and left, Nita smiled at Alyth. "Things are looking up. With Julia backing your shop, that will help to put it on the map."

"If she does."

"Oh, she will. You've caught one of our pack member's atten-tion, and they're not letting you get away."

"Ha! Evander had to rescue his dog that was chasing after mine, so that doesn't really count as an interest in dating."

"But Lana said—"

"That he would ask me, but I will believe that if it happens."

"Will you go out with him?"

Alyth smiled. "Sure. I haven't dated in ages."

"I thought maybe Cal Sutherland would ask you out." Nita started unpacking some boxes of merchandise.

"No way. He's only interested in one thing—stud fees."

"Well, a guy that rescues his dog and yours, in the process, has to be a good guy."

"That's true." Alyth was working on the computer, taking care of some orders from America.

They had several more sales and then she realized it was time for lunch. "Hey, I'll go make us our favorite sandwiches after I feed Skye and take her out."

"On a leash, right?"

Alyth groaned. "You know it." She left through the back door into the house and greeted Skye. "How are you feeling? Like you're full of puppies yet? And they're little deerhound pups, right?" Skye was wagging her tail vigorously. Alyth took her out on a leash, hoping she'd mind her. Of course, as soon as she led her outside, Skye looked in the direction of the gate on the side of the house. Alyth took her that way just to make sure it was secured. "Ha! Locked and you're not getting out that way. Again."

Then she fed Skye and let her out one last time before she began making egg and cheese sandwiches and heather tea for lunch. She ate hers, then relieved Nita so she could eat lunch at the house and keep Skye company a little while longer. Deerhounds loved human companionship. Despite how big they were, they weren't outdoor dogs. They were house dogs just like cute little fluffy toy dogs.

The rest of the afternoon, they continued to be busy, and

even Julia came by to drop off some of her autographed books and a sign. "If you don't want to do this, just tell me, but I'll let everyone know where to get the books on my site if you're alright with the arrangement. Also, if you would like, we could have a book signing when I have a new release."

"Oh, aye, that's just what I figured." Alyth helped set up a table by the window and placed the sign in the window. She was really thrilled to have the extra publicity for her shop, and she was glad to help out Julia also.

"I should have mentioned that half of the profits for the sale of the books go to the shop."

"Thanks, but it's no problem at all. I'm fine with just doing it for you," Alyth said, figuring the books would bring more shoppers and they might sell some other things at the same time.

"Nonsense. Half the proceeds over the cost are yours. Has Evander dropped by yet?" Julia asked.

"Uh, no." Alyth hoped everyone wasn't pressuring him to come see her. She thought just his sister Lana had been.

"I'm sure he will soon. I need to get back to writing. I haven't quite made my word count for the day yet. Ian and his brothers were sword fighting again for me so I would get my scene right this morning and then they got carried away. That's what they were doing when you and Evander returned to the keep with the dogs."

Alyth and Nita laughed.

Then Julia placed an order for Christmas, even though it was months from now. "I like to get my shopping done early."

"Oh, aye, me too." Alyth was so happy that Skye had run away this morning, despite what could come of the pups, just so she could make all these new sales connections.

Julia was soon on her way with an armful of packages and Nita smiled at Alyth. "Can you have Skye, the adventuress, search out another wolf pack so we can get even more business?"

Alyth laughed. "We were lucky this came of it." She glanced at the clock. "Time for closing, and I've got to get ready for Cal's arrival."

"More deerhound loving."

"Yeah, since Magnus is such a stud, as far as with other deerhounds he has been bred to, and the first one to mount Skye, I'm hoping he's going to be the daddy. I'll see you in the morning. Have a nice night."

"I'm sure he is. And you have a great night too!" Nita left the store and got into her car and drove off as Alyth locked the front door to the shop and turned out the lights, then returned to the house.

Skye greeted her with enthusiasm and Alyth put her on her leash to take her out again. She figured she would have a grilled chicken sandwich for dinner tonight after Cal left. She saw his truck pull up and park and Skye yanked at her leash to go greet him. Not Cal, but the stud muffin with him.

"Come on, Skye. You can see Magnus on the porch like before." It was enclosed with a view of a creek, an ancient stone dike, and woods. A really pretty setting for her home and shop. She was a little way out of town, which she preferred, and she had a large parking area for tour buses to bring their patrons for a little Scottish shopping excursion. Also bathrooms for them to use. She always made a fair amount of money off the tourists, but she still had some privacy out here away from the village.

Cal came to the side entrance where everyone came to see her when she was at home, and she opened the door and let him and his deerhound in. Skye and Magnus couldn't wait to greet each other, and they sure didn't need any instruction on what to do. And they weren't going to move to the patio either. Right here in the dining room was good enough for them.

Alyth didn't know why it embarrassed her that the two of them were having such a good time. She supposed it was because she had never bred dogs before. Cal was an old hand at it, so he just folded his arms and watched them.

"Would you like something to drink?" she asked.

Cal shook his head. He was all business. This was about one thing—providing stud service and nothing else and then he was on his way. From what Nita told her, who was more in the know, Cal wasn't seeing anyone in particular, and certainly wasn't mated. Alyth wondered how Evander would have acted toward her if his dog had been a deerhound instead and she had a contract with him to service Skye. Would he have asked her out on a date?

She scoffed at herself. Everyone said he was going to ask her, but she suspected he was being forced to do so, if he even followed through.

Then she heard someone pull up in her parking lot. She never got unexpected visitors at night, though one time a tour group coordinator begged her to open her shop when their bus had broken down earlier, and they were late getting there. Everyone had been so upset about the breakdown, that she was agreeable. She hadn't had anything better to do and she'd made a lot of money that night and she had been delighted that the tourists had been so grateful to her. Plus, she'd felt badly for them getting stuck in the middle of nowhere on a broken-down bus.

She went to the door and peered out. Evander? He was just sitting in his car, waiting for something.

Oh, oh, the MacNeills and the Sutherlands didn't get along. *Great.* Did Evander know that was one of the Sutherlands' vehicles? Uh, yeah, it had a sign on the side about their champion deerhounds. Ugh.

Then Evander got out of his car and came to the door. Her

jaw dropped. She glanced back at Cal. He was still concentrating on the dogs, making sure that the mating was a success.

She hurried outside. "Hey, Evander. I didn't expect you to come here."

"I wanted to apologize for earlier. I mean, about Dillon getting loose."

"Oh." She shrugged, trying to make light of it. She reminded herself Skye could have mixed it up with any dog, and she wouldn't have had such a response from the owner of someone else's dog like she had from Evander and his pack. "I made a mistake in leaving my gate open."

He motioned to Cal's car. "Isn't it a little too late for that?"

"Uh, Magnus already mated with Skye the night before. Did Dillon—"

"Service Skye? Aye. When I reached them, there was no breaking the party up."

She sighed. "Well, they may still be Magnus's pups."

"About that—if they aren't, we'll foot the vet bill."

Her jaw dropped. She wanted to ask if they would take care of the stud fee too! But she figured that was asking for a little too much. "Uh, thank you." She certainly wasn't going to turn him down if the pups were Dillon's and not Magnus's.

"I want to ask you out for dinner. To make up for—all that had happened."

"You don't have to." She didn't want him thinking he had to make amends to her for any reason. It wasn't his fault.

"I want to. After you close your shop? Tomorrow at six? I'll pick you up and take you to a seafood restaurant on the shore?"

She smiled. "Aye, I would like that. Sure. And we leave both the dogs at home."

He chuckled. "That's a given. See you tomorrow night then." He turned to get into his car when Cal came out with his stud dog.

Cal gave Evander a steely-eyed glower.

She waved at Evander, and he saluted her and backed out of the parking lot and drove off down the road. He had looked relieved and thrilled she'd said yes to a date, so it appeared he was the one who had truly wanted to ask her out and not just that everyone else had wanted him to.

"What did *he* want?" Cal asked, getting his dog into his vehicle.

"A date." As if it was any of Cal's business.

"Deerhounds are beneath them. As far as the MacNeill clan are concerned, Irish wolfhounds are the noblest of breeds. You know the MacNeill family came from Ireland originally."

As if they weren't Scottish enough for her.

"So did many of my people."

That shut Cal up.

"I was thinking that I might take a puppy instead of cash for the stud fee. Think on it. Tomorrow night, I'll see you for the last breeding."

Shoot, she forgot about that. "Sure, at—"

"Six, same time as tonight. I'll be here." Then Cal left.

Fine. Evander could come and wait for Cal's dog to do his duty and then she'd have a date with Evander. That should work perfectly. After a two-year relationship had ended with a wolf in Edinburgh, part of the reason why she'd moved out here, she didn't want to care about a wolf like that again and not go forward. Which was why she had finally given him the ultimatum of mating her or ending the relationship. He chose to leave her.

She did have the niggling worry—what if Cal was right? That if she ever mated someone who was kin to the MacNeills who raised Irish wolfhounds, would he love Skye like she did? She knew she was getting way ahead of herself on that, but wolves tended to think in terms of whether a wolf was right for them since they usually didn't take long to recognize they were the right ones for each other. She guessed with Roger, her ex, she had been ignoring the part about how they hadn't really been meant for each other and had stayed with him way too long.

Her thoughts were all over the place and she thought about Cal again. She desperately wanted to give Cal a puppy in lieu of the cash fee and would have jumped at the chance if she knew for sure the puppies, if Skye had any, were Magnus's!

3

"Did you ask her out on a date?" Lana asked Evander when he arrived back at Argent Castle for dinner.

"Aye, you know I said I would." He took his seat next to her in the great hall and one of the long tables.

"I was afraid you would get cold feet."

"Not me. Cal Sutherland was there though." Sure, Evander had been afraid Alyth might say no after what had happened between Dillon and her dog, but he'd had every intention of asking her out.

His sister's jaw dropped.

"Stud service."

Lana frowned. "For her deerhound?"

Evander laughed. "Yeah, I would hope so."

Looking puzzled, Lana frowned. "But Dillon already had his way with her."

"The deerhound, aye."

"Och, you are impossible, Brother."

Ian, Julia, and Ian's brothers walked over to the table to learn what had happened with Alyth, Evander suspected.

"Did you get a date?" Cearnach asked him, the others all waiting to hear the news.

Evander sighed. "Of course I got a date."

"And you offered to pay the vet bill," Ian said.

"Aye, but Cal Sutherland was there with his champion stud dog Magnus, and you know what that means."

Everyone waited to hear more.

"The puppies Skye might have could be Magnus's." Evander didn't think he needed to spell it out.

"Oh, well, if that's the case," Guthrie said, "we won't need to pay the vet bill. She'll have pure bred deerhounds she can sell, and she would have been paying the bill anyway, just like she would pay for the stud fee."

"We'll keep an open mind about it," Julia said. "Let's eat."

Lana moved over a couple of seats so she could sit closer to Heather and so that Cearnach and Duncan could sit on either side of Evander at the table. He knew he was going to get the third degree.

"I can't believe none of us met her before," Cearnach said, as the haddock, potatoes, bread, and salads were served.

"She apologized for trespassing." Evander began eating his haddock.

"She can trespass here anytime." Callum, one of Heather's brothers said, sitting on the other side of Duncan and took a bite of his bread.

Oran chuckled. "Now you wish you had been taking care of Dillon." He was sitting between Callum and their other brother, Jamie.

"Don't you?" Callum asked his brother.

Oran smiled and Evander knew he would have wished it too, but he wasn't going to say. "So what do you think? Do you have a chance with her, Evander?"

"She said yes to a date, didn't she?" Evander figured that was a good start.

"Aye, as long as Cal isn't any competition," Oran warned.

"Cal isn't any competition." At least Evander didn't think so.

"Except he has the right breed of dog to mate with Alyth's." Callum drank some of his wine.

"True. But Cal is all business when it comes to their deerhounds. I doubt she would agree to a date with me if she was interested in seeing him and he'd shown any interest back."

"After seeing you there, do you think he'll change his mind and want to see her?" Callum buttered another slice of bread.

"Maybe." Evander had considered that since Cal was also an alpha male.

"Do we need to give you some tips on how to get and keep a lass?" Jamie was unmarried too, so how would he know how to make inroads with a lovely lass?

"Save the lass—or in this case—her dog. Love her dog and she'll love you." Julia had good advice. Then she leaned over and kissed Ian. He kissed her back and didn't offer any of his own sage advice. He might have figured it could get him into trouble with his mate.

Evander had kind of goofed on that part of the challenge. He loved dogs. All dogs, really. But he had a penchant for Irish wolfhounds, having been raised with them from birth. The deerhounds looked similar to the wolfhounds, but they were slenderer like a greyhound, not as muscular, not as tall. Both had wiry coats and tails, but the wolfhound's tail curved slightly. The deerhound's tail nearly reached the ground. And the deerhound's ears were set high and folded back, but the wolfhound's ears were small and carried like a greyhound's ears. The wolfhounds were courageous and calm and loved to be around kids and family—as wolves or human. It didn't matter to them. They were much too serene to be a good guard dog. The deerhounds were also gentle and sweet, but extremely agile with their slimmer features. They were easygoing and loved their families. But with his comment spoken out loud to Dillon at the loch within hearing distance of Alyth about not mixing it up with a deerhound, he figured he had kind of cooked his goose.

He wasn't going to mention it to the others though. Knowing now that Alyth was trying to breed her dog to a champion deerhound stud dog, Evander hoped Dillon hadn't screwed that up for her. And Evander hoped he wasn't wrong about Cal wanting to date her.

"HEY, EVANDER," Duncan said, pounding on his cottage door later that night. "Are you awake?"

"Barely." Evander got out of bed and threw on a pair of boxer briefs, then went to the door and unlocked and opened it. "What's wrong?" He figured it had to be an issue with the dogs.

"Dillon was missing before bed check. Ian was rough-housing with the dogs before he went to bed. I guess the gate was still open. You know we never have to worry about the dogs running off."

"Not until a deerhound in heat showed up."

"Right. Ian told me to settle them down and put them to bed and not to disturb you because you had a busy day and night ahead of you, but I figured you would want to do it."

"Aye, I'll find Dillon," Evander said.

"Do you need more of us to help you search for him?" Duncan asked.

"No, he won't have gone far. If I can't find him, I'll call up the troops. No sense in a bunch of us missing out on our sleep unless I don't locate him. I'll just go as a wolf." Evander grabbed a leash and handed it to Duncan. Then he pulled off his boxer briefs and shifted into his wolf.

Duncan handed the folded-up leash to him so Evander could carry it in his mouth, then Duncan closed the door behind him. "Just howl if you need help."

Evander gave a muffled woof and tore off to the castle gates to smell where Dillon had run, then raced off to find him. Dillon had run all over the place, following Skye's scent all the way from the castle to the loch. Luckily not to Bird Island again. Evander listened as a wolf, his ears twitching back and forth. He didn't hear any sounds. Not of birds disturbed in their nests or anything. Evander sniffed around the shore further, smelling both Skye and Dillon's scents and Alyth's too—of summer warmth and femininity, of a female wolf, high tension, and disappointment.

Okay, boy, you better not have followed Skye's scent all the way to her home. Then Evander found droplets of water where Dillon had shaken the excess water off after taking a swim and checking for Skye on the island. Not finding her, Dillon was hot on her trail that she must have left, coming from her house through the MacNeill woods.

The good news was he could track Dillon as a wolf and find him. And at this hour, Skye should be happily asleep wherever she normally slept. Hopefully inside Alyth's house under lock and key.

Evander kept thinking he would catch up to Dillon, but he must have been gone for some time before Duncan realized he wasn't in the kennel. At least Dillon's litter mate hadn't sneaked off too. Usually when one did, his brother did also.

When Evander reached the edge of the woods, the scents were in the pastureland where the Highland cows grazed. Dillon had easily cleared the four-foot fence. Then Evander was over it and still tracking both dogs' scent trails that they'd left behind—Skye's from earlier, Dillon's from recently. And Evander knew just where Dillon was headed—for Alyth's house. This was still the fastest way to go, unless he'd known where Dillon was going in the first place, and he could have driven there. As a wolf, he could move even faster than if he'd tried to manage as a human racing through the woods and catapulting over fences. He'd never tried leashing Dillon and then walking him home as a wolf though. That was the only thing he could think of doing. No way did he want to wake Alyth and have her drive him and Dillon home. He hoped he could do this without disturbing her and before she ever learned of it.

And then? Dillon was in the proverbial doghouse.

At least Scottish deerhounds rarely barked when someone got close to their home, so Skye, hopefully, wouldn't wake Alyth over Dillon's visit. Irish wolfhounds didn't bark alarms either. So Evander had a good chance of moving Dillon from the area without too much trouble, he thought.

Evander was nearly to her house, his heart racing and his tongue hanging out, panting up a storm. He paused, confused, when he didn't see Dillon at Alyth's gate or her side door to the house.

Had he cleared the six-foot fence? There were no other homes or businesses from which people could see what Evander was up to. Dillon could either shift and open the gate or jump the fence. He figured he would do it the easy way and open the gate. As soon as he shifted, he tried that, but it was locked!

So then he shifted and leaped over the fence and found Dillon wagging his tail like crazy and trying to get in through the wolf door to the house, scratching and clawing.

"Dillon," Evander said after he shifted, his voice low and dark with command. He was headed for him, leash in hand, figuring Dillon wouldn't run off. Not when the object of his desire was inside the house, whimpering. He hoped Alyth was sleeping through all this.

Then the porch light came on and the curtain in a window opened. Alyth was standing there wearing a long, blue T-shirt featuring a red furry Highland cow and her calf pictured on it. Alyth was looking at him, her lips parted in surprise. What could Evander do but smile, hold up the leash, and motion to Dillon, the cause of all the trouble. He finally managed to get the leash on Dillon and Evander put the leash in his mouth, then shifted.

He glanced at the window. Alyth was still watching him. Evander considered the fence. He was certain he couldn't leap over the fence with Dillon in tow. The dog would fight him to stay here with Skye.

Alyth left the window and he looked at the gate again. Maybe Alyth could open the gate for him at least, and then he would pull Dillon home. He shifted and pulled the leash out of his mouth and was about to knock on her door when she opened it. There was no sign of Skye, thankfully, though Dillon made a mad dash to run into the house.

"No, Dillon, stay." Evander kept a firm hand on the leash and smiled at Alyth. "I wonder if I could ask if you could open the gate for me."

"How come every first encounter we have, you're naked?"

"It all has to do with two horny dogs." He smiled.

She sighed and pushed her dark hair out of her face. "So how often has *this* happened?"

"Never."

"Come in." She sounded tired and slightly annoyed. Maybe a little resigned.

"If I could use your phone, I can call someone at the castle, and they will come and pick me up."

"And then more people would know you were out chasing

Dillon down again? Dressed like that?" She motioned to his nakedness. "I'll drive the two of you home."

At least she was a wolf and wasn't shocked to see him like this. Twice. "Duncan knows. Everyone will be concerned about Dillon and ask me how I got him back anyway, but thanks, I'll take you up on your offer."

He locked her back door, and she gave him a large, blue bath towel. "Hopefully, we won't get stopped."

Evander smiled and wrapped the blue towel around his waist. "Where's Skye? Forget it. I hear her in that room whimpering."

"She normally sleeps in her bed in my bedroom, but she left the bedroom to whimper at the back door when she heard that her former lover was visiting. I shut her up in my bedroom. Hold onto Dillon. I need to go to my room to get dressed."

"Aye, I've got him."

BUT ALYTH DIDN'T HAVE control of Skye right away. She grabbed her collar as Skye frantically tried to reach Dillon. For a few minutes, the two wild dogs were trying to get to each other before Alyth finally managed to get Skye under control and she made her stay in the bedroom until she could shut her bedroom door. "Be out in a sec."

She hurried to get dressed in a pair of pants and boots, then a shirt.

She couldn't believe Dillon had escaped the castle grounds and had come all the way here in search of Skye. She was glad he had safely reached her place. Not only that, she couldn't believe that Evander had followed Dillon here as a wolf. She was relieved no one had seen him as a wolf, at least she hoped no one had. He was a beautiful black wolf with a white muzzle and white and gray hairs in his coat around his chest and body, and big, big feet. Just beautiful.

When he'd leaped over her fence, she'd held her breath, glad he'd made it just fine. She would have opened the gate for him, but she hadn't realized Dillon was even in the yard at first. She'd missed seeing Dillon jumping over the fence. That would have been a sight too.

She'd wondered why Skye had woken her, excited about something. A male dog? Sure.

She had to fight Skye to keep her in the bedroom before she got out again. Then Alyth closed the door and went with Evander and his dog to the car. She would have taken hold of Dillon so Evander wouldn't lose the towel around his narrow hips, but the dog was too eager to return to the house and the love of his life. At least while Skye was in heat.

Evander lost the bath towel once while he was trying to get an obstinate Dillon in her vehicle, and she stifled a chuckle. It was a sight to behold. The guy was well-built and worth a second glance and more—with or without his clothes.

"Sorry about this," he said on the way back to the MacNeill property. "I never thought Dillon would sneak out beyond the castle walls and follow Skye's scent trail all the way back to your house."

"Is that why you ran as a wolf?" At least the night was still warm so he wouldn't be cold wearing only a towel home.

"Yeah. If I had realized he would run straight to your house following Skye's trail, I could have just driven over here."

"True. No one saw you running as a wolf?"

"No. Everyone was asleep, like all of us should be." He sighed.

She smiled. "Aye, I agree."

"Well, I really am sorry about this."

"Don't be. It's just too bad Dillon wasn't a Scottish deer-hound and Skye could be serviced for free."

Evander chuckled. "We do charge for stud service normally. But not in a case like this."

"Good, because after having to pay Cal's stud fee, I couldn't afford to pay another. The worst thing is, Cal is changing his mind about taking a puppy instead of the money and I can't do it if they're not Magnus's pups, as much as I wish I could."

"Because any pups she might have could be Dillon's."

"Right."

"I wouldn't tell him." Evander smiled at her.

She laughed. "Oh, aye, that's all I need to do is get on the Sutherlands' bad side. I can see him ruining both my dog's chances of having future puppies, if I wanted to do it again, and trying to cause trouble for my shop. Of course, even just dating you could annoy him."

"I'm not calling off our date."

She smiled. "I wouldn't let you."

"Did he say anything about it?" Evander was frowning at her now, looking like a warrior in a towel kilt and nothing else, who was ready to take on the Sutherland singlehanded.

"Only that you had Irish wolfhounds, as if I didn't know, and that they were Irish—not Scottish like the deerhounds. And that the MacNeills were from Ireland to begin with."

"Aye, that they are." Evander looked like he was waiting for her to tell him how she felt about it.

She shrugged. "My people came from Ireland also, a few Vikings in the mix, some Highlanders, and Normans. Not pure-bred at all."

"I'm sure most of us can say the same. If he gives you any trouble at all, just let me know."

She glanced down at the bath towel.

"I'll be dressed better the next time." He winked at her.

She felt her whole body warm with intrigue. There was just something about Evander that made her want to see more of him—and even his charge, Dillon.

When they finally reached the castle, Evander directed her to his cottage. "I live beyond the castle walls. I'll let everyone know I got back fine with Dillon. I'll wash your bath towel and return it to you when I pick you up for dinner."

"Okay, sure, thanks."

He got out of the car and grabbed the back door and Dillon's leash. "Come on, Stud." Then he came around to the driver's side of the car and Alyth rolled down her window.

"See you for dinner," she said.

He smiled. "Aye." He leaned down and pressed his lips against hers.

If she hadn't been sitting down, she would have swooned. His hot lips against hers made hers sing with happiness. Did he feel it too? The world spinning around? The magic? Or was it just that she hadn't kissed a guy in so long? And a wolf? A wolf in her bath towel, the rest of him perfectly naked. Hmm.

He finally broke off the kiss, his blue eyes filled with lust, the corner of his mouth quirking up.

Man, was he a wolf.

"After work then."

She smiled. "Aye." She drove off, glancing in her rearview mirror and saw Evander just standing there in the blue towel, his sexy chest and legs and arms bare, Dillon sitting next to his feet, both of them watching her go. What a hunk. Talk about a stud. And she wasn't talking about the dog.

4

Before Evander could enter his cottage, Duncan came out of it to see him.

"I saw you got a ride home." Duncan looked down at the towel Evander was wearing. "And a towel." He smiled, then greeted a tired Dillon. "Best of all, you got Dillon back. I'll take him to the kennel. You probably are about wiped out. I had to stay here, per Ian's orders, until I knew you both were back safely."

"Thanks. Dillon ran all the way to Alyth's house and jumped the fence."

Duncan shook his head. "And you?" He took hold of Dillon's leash.

"Yeah, me too."

Duncan laughed. "And you got caught at it."

"I sure did. Here I thought I was a lot stealthier than that. Thanks for locking him up. I'll see you in the morning." Evander and Dillon's escapades would be the talk of the pack tomorrow.

But all Evander could think of when Duncan and Dillon were on their way to the castle kennels was the kiss he'd shared with Alyth. She was remarkable, devoted to her dog like he was to the MacNeills' dogs, had a sense of humor when it came to him jumping her fence in the middle of the night as a wolf, and thankfully wasn't irritated with him. He couldn't wait to see her when he took her out to dinner.

He climbed into bed and got a call, figuring it was from Ian, but to his surprise it was from Alyth. "Hey, is everything okay? Skye didn't get out, did she?" He was ready to go and hunt Skye down for Alyth, already out of bed and grabbing his boxer briefs.

"Nay. She's fine. I, uh, just wanted to say that Cal's coming with Magnus to do one more mating. I forgot to mention it to you after all the commotion. I wondered if you would want to come about half an hour later to pick me up for dinner?"

Relieved Skye was safely at home, he ditched the boxer briefs and climbed back into bed. "No. I'll be right on time, like I said I would be." And he was ready for another kiss. No matter what, he wanted to make sure Cal didn't ask her out because someone who worked for the MacNeill clan wanted to date her. He realized taking her out for dinner as an apology for what had happened between Dillon and Skye was already evolving into something more.

"Okay, well, I don't want the two of you fighting or anything."

"I'll be on my best behavior." Unless Cal wasn't.

"All right. Night," she said, sounding dreamy and happy.

"Night, lass." They ended the call, and he rested the phone against his bare chest and looked up at the ceiling. He could still feel the heat of her full lips pressed against his mouth. This would be a day—and a night—to remember.

EARLY THE NEXT MORNING, Alyth headed out to her car so she could go to the grocery store before she had to open her store.

She glanced at a car sitting at a shop across the street—a quaint little Scottish bakery, that wasn't open yet. A red Kia Picanto. It wasn't the owner's. And she swore it had been there the morning she'd found her gate open, and Skye had run off to find her hot doggy, Dillon.

She had an uneasy feeling in her gut about it. Maybe it was the owner's relative's car, or someone who just started working for them and the person wasn't there that often. Like a part-time baker or something. But she couldn't help worrying about the car. She didn't see anyone in it though. She called Nita and said, "Hey, I know you're not supposed to be here for another hour, but could you sit with Skye until the shop opens? I'll pay you for it."

"No problem at all. Is she okay?"

"Yes. I was going to get some groceries and I know I'm just being silly about this, but there's a strange car parked across the street at the bakery and...I don't know. I just feel worried about her being alone."

"I'll be right over," Nita said.

"Thanks." Alyth was not prone to feeling paranoid. She didn't want to feel like that ever. But she just couldn't risk any harm coming to Skye. She waited for Nita to arrive, and she gave her a hug. "Thanks so much for doing this for me."

"I looked for the red car. It was gone."

"Okay, good." Alyth did think it was odd that if someone meant to do anything untoward, they would use a red car to do it. Why not something drabber? Less noticeable? "I'll be back shortly."

"All right. I'll watch over her." Nita greeted Skye, giving her a hug.

Alyth gave Nita a hug too. "Thanks." She left the house and saw that the red car was gone. Okay, so maybe it was no big deal. Then again, why would it come and then disappear after Alyth returned to the house? Like the driver, though she hadn't seen one, had realized she had seen it and left.

She got into her car and drove to the grocery store, watching for any sign of the red car, but she didn't see one that looked like the one parked at the bakery shop. Thankfully, whoever it was wasn't following her.

WAY BEFORE EVANDER was ready to wake up, he dressed and headed to the castle to take care of the dogs, walk them, feed them, walk them, then have breakfast with several of his clan members.

Cook had taken off on vacation, so Heather and Evander's sister were preparing the morning meal. Heather was the proud owner of Ye Olde Highland Pie Shoppe in the village near the MacNeill's Argent Castle, but it wasn't open this early, and she always helped with breakfast when Cook was away. Others were serving the meals, but as soon as Evander went to take a bite of his eggs, Lana and Heather joined him.

"So, I heard about last night." Lana was the baker at Heather's pie shop, and they were the best of friends.

"I'm sure everyone did."

"Duncan isn't much for spreading tales, but he had to tell everyone about this. Just in case anyone had the idea to ask Alyth out on a date. They're too late." Lana smiled at Evander. "What are you going to do about the puppies if they turn out to be Dillon's?"

"The MacNeills only raise purebred Irish wolfhounds, take them to shows, breed them, keep the puppies from some of the litters, sell others."

"Aye. I didn't ask you what the MacNeills did. I know what they do. What I want to know is what *you're* going to do about the puppies Skye has if they're not purebred deerhounds?" Lana was not going to let him off the hook as far as what he planned to do about it.

"Why would *I* have anything to do with them?"

"Dillon got away from you on your watch."

Evander shook his head. "I'm sure Alyth can sell them. Maybe not for as much as she had planned, but still, they'll be good-looking and good-natured dogs. It might even be difficult to tell if the puppies are purebred or not."

"You're not advocating letting on that they're purebred if they're not, are you?" Lana asked.

"Nay, you know me better than that. I'm just saying that someone could get a less expensive dog that looks and behaves like our gentle giants—either of them. They won't have the UK Kennel Club registered papers that say they're one or the other, not unless they are truly Magnus's pups. Ironically, he's now saying he will take a pup instead of the money for a stud fee."

Heather and Lana smiled.

"She should go for it," Heather said.

"I agree." Lana forked up some of her haggis.

"I thought you were against letting on that they were purebred, if they are not." Evander was amused at his sister's about-face.

"In Sutherland's case, I would make an exception. Though I wouldn't want Alyth to get into trouble for it when he learned the truth." Lana finished off her eggs.

"She can order kits from her vet to do DNA testing on the newborn puppies, just by obtaining cheek-swab samples. She just has to separate the pups from the dam for about half an hour, make sure they don't have milk in their mouths, and then swab them." Evander hadn't seen his sister so interested in the breeding of dogs ever. That was his job, as far as Lana was concerned.

She loved the puppies after one of their dams had some, like everyone else did, but Lana had never cared before about how that came about.

"Do you feel like an expectant father?" Heather asked.

He smiled at her. He never thought anyone would be asking him that question. Oddly enough, he did kind of feel that way about Skye's puppies, if she was going to have any. He guessed it was because it wasn't supposed to have happened and he was partly at fault for it. And because he really liked Alyth and her dog.

"I think they would make a cute couple, don't you?" Heather asked.

"Dillon and Skye? I think they kind of are." Lana drank some of her tea.

"Nay, Alyth and your brother." Heather shook her head at Lana.

Ian and his brothers and Julia joined them at the table.

"So," Julia said, "how's our new momma coming along?"

LATE THAT AFTERNOON, Nita wrapped up another tartan blanket and handed it to the customer, smiling. But as soon as the customer thanked her and left the shop, Nita caught Alyth looking at the clock on the wall—again. "You know what they say about a watched clock."

Alyth hadn't meant for Nita to catch her at it—again. Then again, Nita had been watching her a lot lately. "A watched kettle never boils."

"Same thing. Glancing at the time constantly won't make it pass any faster." Nita smiled. "Are you looking forward to your date with Evander? I didn't want to bring it up, but I smelled an Irish wolfhound had come here last night and...Evander?"

Alyth let out her breath. "Aye. I'm looking forward to the date and Dillon got loose again. Evander had to come for him."

"He had to track him down?"

"Aye."

"You kissed him this time! He wouldn't let you get away for a second time without a kiss!" Nita smiled broadly. "God, he's so much better than your ex. Roger isn't half the hunk, and he totally had a commitment phobia. Which meant the two of you weren't the ones for each other. Wolves just don't delay committing to each other unless there is something that's keeping them apart."

"Aye. I agree." Alyth couldn't help but blush. She hadn't ever gotten so interested in a wolf like this and it could cause problems, she thought, because of the breed of dogs they both loved —similar, but not the same.

The business picked up then and they'd really kept busy all day. Several customers had even bought Julia Wildthorn's autographed books. Not just the newer books, but some of her earlier releases. In fact, one of the women on a bus tour picked up seven of the books in the series Alyth had on display, telling her friends on the tour that they were more valuable because they were signed by the author, which had encouraged more sales.

Alyth figured she should contact Julia to let her know to bring more books to the store. But then she figured, since Evander was coming to see her anyway, he could just bring some with him. Still, she called Julia to ask if she had any more books she could send over.

"Hi, Julia, we sold twenty-two of your books today."

"Ohmigod, really?"

"Aye. The ladies on the tour buses want something to read from Scotland for their plane trips back home and they were excited to have signed editions. Evander is coming by to take me out to dinner after closing. If Evander and you don't mind, you could send along some more books with him. We can keep some in stock in the storeroom also."

"I'll certainly do that. And thanks!"

"You're so welcome. Nita and I have been talking them up when we have a chance, but they've been pretty much selling themselves on their own anyway. I've got to go. I have more customers."

"Thanks, I'll get in touch with Evander, and he'll bring some more over."

Then they ended the call and Alyth and Nita talked with the members of a new tour group. She was glad so many came in here. She'd set up a place on one wall of the store for drinks and snacks that were highly popular too and packages of tea and herbs and honey made locally.

Before closing, Evander arrived. She hadn't expected him to come before they closed. She hoped he hadn't felt obligated to hurry up with whatever he had been doing just to bring some of Julia's books to sell, though most everyone in the pack was eager to do what their pack leaders wanted them to do. Maybe he was just a little eager to see Alyth too.

What she hadn't expected was to see him carrying the blue bath towel he'd worn home in the middle of the night. She had forgotten he said he was going to wash it and bring it back to her.

Nita's smile widened and she gave Alyth a look that said she needed a further explanation of why Evander was bringing one of Alyth's bath towels to the shop. He set the box of books on the floor and Alyth grabbed the bath towel and put it behind the counter as if hiding the evidence, making her look guiltier than before. She really hadn't wanted to mention to Nita that for a second time, she'd been faced with the naked Highlander.

Alyth was sure Nita would have loved being there at the time.

Evander helped Alyth set up the display, which she appreciated. She hadn't expected him to assist her. Luckily, Nita was busy with a customer, or she would have been watching everything Alyth and Evander were doing. Wolves were curious like that.

Once they had finished setting up the books, Evander carried the box of extra books into the storage room.

Nita said, "Hey, I'll close up if you want to go, Alyth."

"Sure, thanks." Alyth didn't want Evander to have to hang around the shop until she closed, and Nita was just finishing up with a customer. Carrying the freshly washed bath towel, Alyth led Evander into the house through the back door of the shop. "Would you like something to drink? A beer? Soda? Water?"

"I'll take a beer, thanks." In the meantime, Skye was eagerly greeting him, smelling the dog scents on his clothes. "I'll take her out, if you would like me to."

"Aye, that would be great. Be sure and take her out on her leash though." Alyth pointed to a rack of brass hooks on the wall near the door where Skye's leash was hanging.

"My thought exactly. You do know about DNA testing for the pups, right?"

"Aye, I looked it up yesterday."

"I can help you with it after they're born."

She smiled at him.

"I can help you find homes for them, whether they're Magnus's or Dillon's pups also."

She took a relieved breath. "Thanks. I would appreciate that too."

"Okay, I'll be back in a minute."

She brought out a beer and watched Evander as he threw a ball for Skye in the backyard. He was talking away to her, and

Skye was eager to play, just like being a puppy again, her leash trailing behind her. She fetched the ball several times before he took hold of her leash—he appeared to like to live dangerously, because if she got out, he was chasing her down—and bringing her back inside.

Evander was really good with Skye and Alyth was glad to see it. And she was really thrilled he wanted to help her with the pups! He had to be an expert at it, and this was a first time for her.

"Thanks for playing with Skye. I usually have the wolf door unlocked so she can come and go as she pleases, until she came in heat."

"Yeah, the big dogs need a lot of exercise." He took a swig of his beer.

"Do you have any dams who are about to have puppies?"

"One. Do you want to come see her? She's due any day now. A radiograph revealed she has twelve puppies."

"Oh, how wonderful. I would love to." Alyth would love to see how things worked at the kennel and glean more good information for breeding Skye in the future, if things worked out this time. Maybe it wouldn't be such a good idea. But she wanted to see more of the operation Evander had in any event. "Don't you have to watch her?"

"Someone checks on her throughout the day if I'm not there. We have a teen who sleeps in the kennel at night for early warning if we need it."

"Oh, good."

Cal pulled up into the parking area and she wasn't sure what to do. Evander made it easy for her. "I'll go out back and sit on your patio and drink my beer until you're ready to have dinner with me." He took his beer outside and Skye wanted to go with him, until Alyth opened the front door and let Cal and Magnus in.

Skye was a total traitor, her affections for Evander completely switching to Magnus. But Alyth was so appreciative for Evander being so considerate.

"I see Evander is back," Cal said, his tone of voice disapproving.

"Aye, we're going on a date." She wasn't about to hide that from Cal. Even if it was none of his business.

"Have you decided if you would prefer a puppy or paying the cash fee?" Cal asked, as Magnus and Skye got to the business of mating.

"Can we wait until after the puppies are born, maybe when they're about two weeks old?" Alyth had to get the test on the pups back to make sure of what they were.

She even wondered how Skye would react with raising pups. She'd read where some dams weren't good mothers—they wouldn't stay with their puppies to feed them or keep them warm, too much of a "baby" of their own and wanted all their owner's attention instead.

Cal gave Alyth a calculated smile. "You want to see how cute the puppies are first."

She cast him a sweet smile back, acting as though she was a sentimental sap, when in reality, she wanted to ensure the pups were Magnus's first. "Would that be all right with you?"

"Sure, though they won't look like much when they're first born. We usually take pick of litter between six to eight weeks."

"Oh, okay, then that will work." Though she really hadn't wanted him to know if the pups were his dog's or Dillon's.

"Is this your first date with Evander?" Cal asked.

She was surprised Cal would ask. "Aye."

"How did you meet?"

Talk about a double-edged sword when she'd met him while Evander's dog was servicing hers. "His sister comes in here to shop. So do several of the ladies with the MacNeill clan." None

of the members of the Sutherland clan did and she had never
been affiliated with any of the clans so she was glad she had
mentioned that.

"Ah."

She hadn't said how that had led to her meeting Evander,
but she wasn't about to tell Cal the real story. She glanced down
at Skye who was sleeping next to Magnus now.

"Well, we're done here. If you have any other questions
about breeding or when the puppies come, just give me a call,"
Cal said.

"Thanks, I will." *Not.* She was really surprised to hear him
even offer. Before, it was strictly, breed the dogs and leave. Cash
for the stud service, nothing else. Was he trying to show that he
was just as nice as Evander was?

Cal was all show now. Evander had been genuinely nice
from the beginning. If she had any breeding questions that she
wanted to know the answers to, she would ask Evander. If Cal
had been friendlier to her in the beginning, she might have felt
differently. Cal had such a high opinion of his dogs, and even
had to really check over her pedigree to make sure Skye was
worthy of being serviced by one of Cal's stud dogs before he
would agree. Since she had purchased Skye from an American
breeder, Skye had different bloodlines and therefore it helped to
prevent inbreeding with Cal's own bloodlines, which was why
he said he would do it when Skye was an unproven dam.

Cal finally left with Magnus and then Alyth took Skye
outside on a leash. "Are you ready for dinner?"

"You bet," Evander said, all smiles.

He was so sweet and Alyth was so into Evander already.

They left Skye in Alyth's bedroom and Evander and Alyth
walked outside to his car. She glanced in the direction of the
bakery, but there wasn't any red car there. The bakery was
closed for the night.

5

W hile Evander and Alyth were having dinner at the local seafood restaurant, he ordered Merlot to go with their meals. "I heard Cal offer to give you advice about Skye with regard to her having puppies."

"I would rather ask you about your experiences. He wasn't forthcoming with me at all in the beginning. Not until he knew you were dating me." Well, Evander might not officially be dating her per se, as this was their only date. But because he offered her a chance to see the Irish wolfhound who was ready to birth her puppies, Alyth thought he wanted to get to know her better. She forked up some of her haddock. "Have you always worked with the dogs?"

"Since I was little. Lana and I were orphaned when our dad drowned on a fishing trip in rough seas and our mother drowned when she tried to rescue a child in a swiftly flowing river. At least the boy was rescued. My dad and mom worked for the MacNeill clan so we were still at home with the pack. Another couple took us in. I've always had an infinity toward animals, so when I was old enough, Ian's dad put me to work feeding the dogs and I learned how to obedience train them.

From there, I began showing them, taking some of them to obedience trials, the ones that were better suited for winning, and breeding them. They've done really well."

"I'm sorry about your parents. Mine are gone too. A robbery gone wrong. I had always wished I'd been there for them."

He took hold of her hand and caressed it. "I'm sorry to hear about your parents too. We have such long lives unless they're cut short like that."

She loved how he had reached out to her to comfort her about her loss. "I know, right? Sometimes it seems like we're invincible until we're not." She leaned over and kissed his cheek to show she felt something for him. "That's wonderful about the dogs you take care of. I couldn't decide on which breed of dog to get at first. We had always had dogs while I was growing up, and when Missy died—she was a mix of everything, wonderfully sweet—I wanted to have another. Then a friend of mine from America was living in Scotland and she had Scottish deerhound pups. I fell in love with the friendliest little female pup. The mother was a champion as well as the father. Since the pups were double champion sired, I thought I might try to breed Skye when she was old enough. My shop has done okay, but I thought I might bring in some extra money with the sale of a litter of puppies."

"As to the pups, they can sell for six hundred to eight hundred apiece, even for mixed breeds, especially since the two breeds are so similar. Dillon's still a champion."

She smiled, hoping Evander was right. She could imagine all this just costing her money and not breaking even.

"So if you had—" Evander started to say.

"Don't tell me. I already did that—calculated how much I could make and then Dillon came into the picture."

Evander chuckled. "Sorry about that. I've never seen you at any of the Scottish festivals, or just around and about."

"I just moved here from Edinburgh and opened the shop. Nita has been a friend for years, and she actually moved here with me to get out of the city too and work for me. Neither of us had any family to speak of—old clan wars had eliminated her family. We just needed a change. I had a shop in Edinburgh that did well, but no wolf packs around." She paused, needing to mention Roger, she felt. "Plus, I'd ended a relationship that I'd been in for two years. My ex wasn't ever going to commit, and I was ready for leaving the city for good." She hoped she didn't sound like she was rebounding!

He smiled a little, looking really wolfish. She loved it.

She continued, "Since I moved here, I just haven't tried to meet anyone. I've been too busy with the shop. Then I met Cal —just for breeding purposes, and realized he was a gray wolf too. I was so surprised, but he was all business and that suited me fine. Lana and Heather had come in to check out our shop, and that's when I learned the MacNeill clan at Argent Castle was also made up of gray wolves."

"I can't believe that Lana or Heather didn't tell us about you."

Alyth laughed. "I'm sure they felt sorry for us the first time that they came in. We were still trying to set things up and everything was in disarray. We wanted to open quickly and start making some money, though I'd made a lot of money on the sale of my other business and the merchandise in Edinburgh."

Smiling, Evander shook his head. "Then I just got lucky that Dillon took off like he did."

"You sure did."

Evander laughed and clinked his wine glass with hers.

When they were done with dinner, he took her to walk along the beach to enjoy the sunset. She hadn't expected that, and it was so romantic, the ocean breeze, walking hand in hand with him, his large hand covering hers that was so warm and possessive. "Too bad we can't run as wolves."

"We can. We can go to my place, strip, and take a run on the wild side on the MacNeills' grounds. It's safe there." He sounded eager to take her running as a wolf.

She was excited about it too. "Okay, I'm game." She hadn't run as a wolf in ages, and she wasn't even sure where to go to run where it would be safe here. Nita could too, as long as they had permission. She thought of asking him to drop by her house so she could put something on that was more casual, but she figured it would take more time and they would strip, shift, run, return, she would dress, and he would take her home. So it wasn't like when Alyth went running after Skye while she was dressed in her miniskirt and boots.

When they arrived at his cottage, he showed her to his spare bedroom and she stripped and shifted, then came out to see him sitting at the door in his wolf coat, waiting for her. He smiled with a wolf grin. She smiled back. He was so cute.

Then he led her through the wolf door, and they tore off together. He took her down the high, winding stone stairs to the beach and then they ran on the sand in their wolf coats, but in a protected environment. This was so much fun as she dug her paws in the sand and raced for the water.

He ran into the water at the edge of the surf, and she splashed happily behind him. She'd envisioned running through the woods like she had to do when she was chasing after Skye, nothing like this. The full moon shown down from the dark sky, reflecting light across the surface of the ocean, practically all the way to the shore, like a path that beckoned to them. The wind blew their fur about and the smell of fish in the air made her want to go fishing—purely a wolf instinct.

She'd had such a nice dinner with Evander, she couldn't imagine it being any nicer than that. But this was wonderful. A way to be herself as a wolf, taking a detour into the waves, snapping at the salty water, then turning to chase after Evander. She found him watching her, his tongue hanging out, his tail giving a vigorous wave. Aye, he knew he'd taken her on the best date a wolf could have. She wagged her tail back. She hadn't had this much fun as a wolf in forever.

They chased each other back and forth in the water, having a blast. First, she would lie down and wait for him to attack, and she would chase him and then he would lie down on his belly as she ran a circle around him in anticipation of the chase.

But then a wolf howled from the direction of the castle and Evander lifted his chin and howled back. He nuzzled her face, then licked it. She licked him back, and then he raced down the beach to reach the stairs. At first, she wondered why anyone would alert him of trouble. Then she wondered if the dam that was about to have pups was having them now!

If so, how long would it take for her to birth all those pups if she truly was carrying a dozen?

Evander raced up the flight of stone stairs from the beach to the castle walkway and she ran just as fast as him until he reached his cottage. He pushed through the wolf door, and she followed. He shifted and headed for his bedroom, saying, "Shadow is having her puppies."

Alyth shifted in the guest room and hurried to dress. "I suspected as much."

"Do you want to watch her?"

"Aye." Alyth hoped this would prepare her for when Skye started to have hers. What a magical way to end this date!

EVANDER WAS glad Alyth had the opportunity to see Shadow give birth to at least some of her puppies. He was afraid, after he'd offered for Alyth to watch the birth, Shadow would have had them while Alyth was at the store when it was open for business.

Or in the middle of the night when Alyth was asleep. Though the birthing on average could go on from six to twelve hours, sometimes even longer, depending upon the number of pups and the ease of delivery. He would have to take Alyth home when she was ready to go and someone else could watch Shadow until he returned.

"Will she be all right with a stranger in there with her while she's having the pups?" Alyth asked.

"Aye, she has had two litters before this and doesn't mind the attention."

"Okay, if you're sure. She's going to be tired, and I just don't want to disturb her."

"She'll be fine. You just let me know when you want to go home. This will take hours."

"Oh, sure. I looked it up for Skye and, depending on how many puppies she has, it could take forever."

The pack leaders Julia and Ian were in the birthing room Evander had set aside for momma and pups. Shadow had a dog door so she could go into the yard to relieve herself, then come back in. Shadow was wearing a collar that would allow only her to go in and out while she was taking care of her puppies. She was a brindle like Dillon, her coat a lighter color than his.

Julia and Ian smiled at Alyth. "Welcome," Ian said quietly.

Julia whispered, "Thanks so much for helping to sell my books."

"You're welcome," Alyth said.

"We'll leave you to do your thing and relieve you when you need a break," Ian told Evander.

Evander nodded and motioned to the chair on the outside of the whelping box for Alyth to sit on while Ian and Julia left. Evander sat down on the stool next to the dam, watching her give birth to the second puppy in the litter. The first one was nursing, already cleaned up, and he took a hemostat and heavy sewing thread, tied off the umbilical cord of the second pup, then cut it with a pair of scissors.

"I'm definitely having you come stay with me when Skye has her puppies," Alyth whispered.

Evander smiled at her, glad to hear it. "Sure, it would be my pleasure." He'd been doing this for so long, it was just second nature.

"Who is the daddy?"

Evander smiled at Alyth.

"Dillon."

"He's a dog, what can I say," Evander said.

"That's for sure."

With a pediatric bulb syringe, he suctioned the new pup's airway, grabbed a towel, and cleaned him up, then put him with the mom and tossed the dirty towel in a laundry basket where another used towel was already sitting.

"I'm going to need a bunch of towels when Skye has her puppies," Alyth said.

"I'll bring all the supplies over that she and the puppies need," Evander said.

Evander put down some more clean newspaper on the floor and smiled at Alyth. She smiled back, but he imagined she felt a little overwhelmed with all she would have to do when Skye's pups were born.

"That one was breech," Alyth whispered, sounding a little worried.

"They can have them either way and it's fine."

"Oh, good."

Three more puppies later, Evander caught Alyth yawning. She had been placing the puppies into a second laundry basket while Mom was pacing before she had the next pup.

"She's all right, isn't she?" Alyth asked.

"Aye. This is just natural."

When Shadow laid down again, Alyth helped put the puppies with their momma again so they could bond and eat and stay warm.

"Are you ready to go home? It's already past midnight," he asked. "Shadow has had only four. She's not even halfway done."

"I want to stay, but I'm useless if I don't get any sleep before I have to work at the shop. But I don't want you to have to leave Shadow while she's still having puppies."

"A couple of Heather's brothers will spell me. I took you out tonight; I'm not having someone else take you home. Besides, I need a break."

She smiled. "You have a very good reason for not taking me home after a date though. Besides, you offered to stay at my house when Skye has her pups and help me with them."

"Aye, but I'm still taking you home." He washed up, then called Jamie. "Hey, do you and Oran want to spell me while I take Alyth home?"

"How many pups has Shadow had?" Jamie asked.

"Four, so it will be a while before she's finished."

"I'll get Oran and we'll be there in a few minutes."

"Jamie and Oran, Heather's brothers, are on their way," Evander told Alyth.

"Okay. Uh, she's having another." Alyth sounded a little panicked.

Evander smiled at her. "All right. We'll take care of this one and then go, if that's all right with you."

"Absolutely." Alyth smiled. "This is miraculous."

"It truly is, and every time is just as miraculous. Would you like to go out to dinner with me after work tomorrow?"

"You are going to be worn out."

"Aye, he is," Jamie agreed as he and Oran walked into the birthing room. "I can take you out."

Evander just chuckled and finished taking care of the pup.

She smiled at the guys. Evander knew she wasn't going for it. "I can fix us dinner at my place," she said to Evander, "but if you need to be here for Shadow, I'll understand."

"We'll take care of her," Oran said. "We have a whole pack who will, so it's no problem. You two can enjoy the time off."

"Thanks," Alyth said.

"Yeah, thanks, guys." Evander patted Shadow on the head, and Alyth had to rub her bony head too, then she and Evander headed out to the cottage and his car. "Thanks for sticking it out with me for so long."

"Oh, this has been great. I wouldn't have missed it for the world. Besides, I needed to learn all I can about it."

They got into his car, and he drove her home. "Well, you were a big help. I had fun. Shadow loved you for taking care of her puppies and when she wanted to pace, keeping them warm, and happy." He hadn't expected to see Alyth sitting on the floor with the puppies in her lap, stroking them. She would be a good momma.

"Is there anything you don't like to eat, or anything you would like that I can fix for us tomorrow night?" she asked.

"It's up to you. I'll eat anything."

"Okay."

It didn't take long for him to reach her place. He got out of his car to walk her to the door. He wanted to kiss her before he left her at her house, to let her know how special she was to him and that he wanted to do a lot more with her. She unlocked the front door and then turned.

"Goodnight, Evander." Then she wrapped her arms around his neck and lifted her face to his.

He wrapped his arms around her waist and pulled her close. And kissed her soft, upturned lips, thinking *this* was a miracle, meeting her the way he had. They were getting serious about this, their lips parted, their tongues exploring, their pheromones sparking, but then they heard Skye woof from her bedroom as if she was telling them they shouldn't forget her.

Alyth pulled her mouth from his. "Tomorrow night, then."

"Yeah, you know it." He kissed her again, and then she went inside where Skye was eager to greet her.

Evander drove home feeling on top of the world.

When he arrived there to help Shadow with more of her pups, his sister came to see him. "You're going to mate her, aren't you?" Lana asked her brother.

"We just met and we're dating."

"Well, just so you know, there are other wolves sniffing around, so don't wait too long or you could miss out."

Evander smiled at his sister. "If you know so much about Alyth, who is making an effort to see her?" He really didn't think anyone else could be or he would have smelled another male around her other than Cal.

"Oran dropped by to see her at the shop to tell her how much he liked her dog."

Now that surprised Evander. Normally when a wolf male or the she-wolf let it be known he or she was dating a particular wolf. Other wolves in the pack would not encroach on the single wolf. Not unless there was a fallout between the pair and then they were fair game.

"And of course then his brothers had to drop by the shop to tell her how sweet and pretty her dog is. I mean, they know you're with her but they're just letting her know that if things don't work out between the two of you, they're definitely interested. And they hope you learn about it—from me—so that you keep up your game with her and don't let her down."

Oh, he had every intention of keeping his game up with her.

6

"Oh, Skye, we've got a real man in our lives now and he's going to help you through your pregnancy." Alyth took Skye out to relieve herself and then brought her back inside. Alyth stripped out of her clothes and took a shower. Skye lay down next to the shower while Alyth was washing up like she always did.

Alyth was so glad she'd met Evander and not just because he could help her with Skye. He was just fun to be with.

She couldn't wait to see him tomorrow night. She couldn't stop thinking about Shadow's pups though, all black with tiny pink feet and tails wagging like crazy as they fed from their momma. They were adorable. Alyth wished she had a huge place where she could keep a whole bunch of them.

"The puppies you smell on me were just as cute as you were when you were a little one, Skye." Alyth got out of the shower and wrapped herself in the towel Evander had used and washed, her own still in the dryer.

She pulled on another of her Scottish T-shirts, a purple thistle decorating it, and she headed for bed, glad she'd gotten to see the puppies being born.

But then she got a call from Rebecca Johnson, her American friend who owned Skye's momma, Princess, and she was thrilled to hear from her. "Hi, Alyth, how are things going with you and the breeding?"

"Ohmigod, you wouldn't believe everything that has gone wrong." Alyth told her all about Skye running off and meeting up with a hot Irish wolfhound that had made her heart pitter-patter.

Rebecca laughed. "Oh, no. That happened once to Princess. Luckily, she didn't have puppies from the union with a German shepherd. At least if Skye has puppies by the stud of an Irish wolfhound, they'll be cute. The dogs look so similar."

"True, but I've bred her to Cal's dog, Magnus, and he doesn't know."

"Oh, yeah. His dog Magnus. He's a good dog. Do you have any more sessions with Cal?"

"No. Hopefully, Skye will have full breed deerhounds."

"Well, I always use a vet, or I would help you out during the delivery."

"No problem, Rebecca. Dillon, the dog that has gotten Skye's attention, comes with a hunk of a handler and he helps the MacNeill clan with delivering the pups. He even showed me how to do it."

"Oh, that's cool. So, uhm, tell me about this stud. The human version."

"He's all wolf. I mean, totally."

Rebecca laughed. "Do you have a picture of him?"

"No. I'll have to take one of him and share with you."

"Before the wedding."

Alyth laughed.

"Well, I hope it all goes well for you on the dog mating. The puppies can be such a joy."

"Thanks. I might have gotten something out of the bargain that I hadn't planned for—a couple of things really."

"A hunk of Scot and a mix of two different gentle giants."

"Right. It's so good to hear from you. When I'm able to learn what I have, I'll let you know." Alyth always felt good after talking with her friend.

"But don't forget to send me a photo of him! The Scottish hunk."

Alyth laughed. Rebecca was looking for one herself.

After Alyth climbed into bed for the night, she got a call from Lana. She hoped everything was alright with Evander.

"We need to have lunch together. I know Evander will be having lunches with you before long, and dinners, every excuse he can make to be with you, but I told him you and I need to get together," Lana said.

Alyth laughed. She hoped it was true, though she didn't have a lunch date with Evander for tomorrow. Just a dinner date.

"Oh, sure, that would be fun." Alyth figured Lana wanted to get to know her better, one on one, without her brother being there.

"Great. Evander said he hadn't made lunch plans with you for tomorrow because he was taking care of Shadow and her pups, but he's having dinner with you, so would lunch work out for you?"

"Yeah. We could have a later lunch and that way I'll make sure that Nita gets her lunch first. She'll feed Skye then too."

"Perfect. I want to do this before you and Evander decide to mate," Lana said.

"You're not going to try and change my mind about him, are you?" Alyth didn't believe it, rather that Lana would try and convince Alyth that her brother was the right one for her.

"Only if you're not sure he's the one for you."

Alyth smiled. "Okay, it sounds like fun."

"I'll pick you up at..."

"Noon. Nita will eat at eleven."

"See you then!"

"I can't wait." Now Alyth figured she should ask questions of his sister to learn all there was to know about Evander.

After they said good night to each other, Alyth called Nita. "I've got a lunch date with Lana at noon so you can have lunch at eleven."

"I always like eating earlier, so that works for me. Sooo, is little sister going to convince you what a great guy her brother is or is she going to tell you all the fun stuff about him?"

"I don't know, but I'm making a list."

Nita laughed. "How come I knew you would?"

Before Alyth was ready for the day to start, it was time to get up the next morning, and she hurried through her routine, dressing, taking Skye out, bringing her in, feeding her, taking her out, bringing her in, and grabbing a scone and a cup of heather tea before she went to the shop to begin working.

Nita came in shortly after Alyth arrived and was putting out merchandise while Alyth was ordering more.

"So, how was it? Did you have a good time at dinner last night?" Nita asked her.

"Aye, and we went for a wolf run, and then I helped with Shadow's puppies. The Irish wolfhound started birthing them while we were on our run."

"Oh, wow, I can't believe it."

"It was really beautiful. Plus, I learned a few things to help me when Skye has her puppies."

Nita smiled. "That's wonderful. I probably shouldn't ask, but you know me, I have to know. Why did the hot Highlander have your bath towel?"

Alyth laughed. She knew she couldn't get away with not telling her about it. After she told her about how Evander, as a wolf, had tracked down Dillon to Alyth's house, Nita laughed.

"Ohmigod, he's priceless and just the one for you, don't you think?"

Alyth smiled.

"Aye, I know that look. You are totally into him already," Nita said.

She was right!

The day was busy, but during a lull in sales, Alyth texted Evander: *How is Shadow doing?*

It took him a few minutes before he texted her back: *She's doing great. All the pups are healthy and thriving.*

I'm so glad to hear it. Okay, got some more customers. I'll see you tonight.

He texted back: *I'm looking forward to it.*

She couldn't wait, but she was eager to have lunch with his sister too. She was kind of surprised he hadn't mentioned it.

After Nita returned to the shop from Alyth's house, once she'd had lunch and taken Skye out and fed her while Alyth managed the shop, Lana arrived to pick up Alyth to go with her to a pie shop.

"Have fun, lassies," Nita said.

"We will, thanks," Alyth said.

"For sure," Lana added.

When they got into Lana's car, Alyth brought out her list and Lana glanced at it and asked, "Don't tell me. You have questions to ask me about Evander?"

Alyth smiled. "I'm a list person. What can I say?"

"Okay, shoot."

"What's his favorite song?"

"What? You're not going to ask who he dated last or when?"

"No. I want to know what his favorite song is."

"'Loch Lomond,' by the Celtic group, Runrig."

"What's his favorite meal?"

Lana smiled. "Salmon. Surely you have some scandalous questions to ask about him."

Alyth chuckled. "No. If I do, I'll ask him."

"Okay, good enough. When we were kids, he tipped over the boat we were in to get me wet."

"No." Alyth was surprised. He seemed so...hero like, not at all like he would dunk his sister while they were in a boat.

"Aye." Lana parked at the pie shop, and they got out. "I have to admit I was giving him a hard time about dating a girl I didn't like. We were fifteen at the time."

They walked into the shop and found seats at a table next to a window. Then they both ordered steak pies and lavender tea.

"So what happened?" Now this was a side of Evander that Alyth had never expected.

"Oh, don't worry. He would never do that to you. Just his sister. Anyway, I kept bothering him about her and he finally just rocked the boat until I fell overboard."

"In a loch?"

"Aye. But the joke was on him. He ended up overturning the boat so much that it filled with water, and he had to swim to shore to empty it out. I mean, it was mostly under water, and he didn't have an easy time of it when he was trying to drag it to shore. I was wringing out my clothes on shore, just smiling at him. It was summer and we were hot, so I didn't mind taking a dip. But I'll have you know when he got the boat to shore, he absolutely couldn't flip it over to empty the water out without my help. Once he apologized to me, I helped him, and we carried the boat home. Of course our parents wanted to know how we ended up looking like a couple of drowned kids and we just made up a story about accidentally tipping over the boat."

Their pies and tea were delivered to their table, and they began to eat.

"What about Evander's girlfriend that you didn't like?" Alyth asked.

Lana laughed. "See? I knew you would want to know about her. It's only natural. She wasn't good for him. I think he felt he had something to prove to me so he kept seeing her until he learned she was seeing someone else. I told him she wasn't good for him. But now you? That's a whole other story. So what do you think of him?"

"He's a dream come true, but I didn't say that." Alyth was afraid Lana would tell her brother that right away. He was, but she shouldn't have mentioned it to Lana.

"What about you and guys you have dated?"

"Well, the last one I dated for quite a while, and then I gave him the ultimatum of mating me or finding someone else."

"You were that serious about him?" Now Lana sounded surprised.

"Yeah, but he definitely wasn't into me. I think for me, it was more that I didn't realize how good things could be until I found a wolf who really meant the world to me."

"You mean my brother."

Alyth smiled. "I didn't say that."

Lana smiled back. "Aye, but that's who you mean." She sighed. "Good. This has been the perfect lunch date. We'll have to do it again sometime, but I suspect Evander's going to want more and more of your free time."

Alyth wondered if he had spoken to Lana about it. How would she know otherwise?

Lana drank some of her tea and put her cup back down. "He doesn't stop talking about you and Skye."

"To you?"

"To everyone! I mean, sure some ask how things are going, besides me, and our pack leaders are really interested, but yeah, to everyone."

"I guess that's always the way it is when wolves are dating in a pack. I've never been in one so this is all new to me."

"Oh, aye, that's the way it is. Of course some of it is that the bachelor males are restless to see where this is going. Are you going to stay with Evander? Or do they have a chance to be with you instead? That's what they're wondering."

Alyth took another bite of her pie. "Well, for now, I have no intention of breaking up a good thing. Evander is the best thing that has happened to me in a good long while."

"I'll tell him so, just in case he's feeling insecure."

"No."

Lana laughed.

Alyth didn't think Evander would feel insecure about anything, but what did she know? After they had their delightful lunch, and Lana dropped her off at the shop, Alyth was afraid Lana would tell Evander everything she had said about him.

"Hey, so how did it go? Did you ask all your questions of Lana?" Nita asked.

"No. We got sidetracked. I asked about the music he liked and his favorite food, but then we went off on a tangent." Where she said way too much about how much she liked Evander. Which was fine if the time seemed appropriate and she said those things to his face, but not if Lana told him all about it.

"Did she tell you how great he was, or detail some of his faults?"

Alyth smiled and shook her head. "She mentioned Evander tipping over a boat they were both in and dunking her."

Nita laughed. "He sounds like he has a great relationship with his sister."

"Aye, but she promised he wouldn't do that to me."

"Of course not. She's his sister. Totally a different scenario."

Then they had some customers and were busy the rest of the afternoon. That night, they said goodbye, and Alyth headed into her house to take Skye out before Evander arrived.

Alyth made grilled chicken breast topped with crumbled goat cheese, sun-dried tomatoes, and lemon basil sauce. Even Skye seemed excited, as if she knew they were having an important guest visiting. When Evander arrived, he had brought Sauvignon Blanc, pink roses, and white lilies, and a box of dark chocolate truffles filled with Scottish cream. She hadn't expected that, and she loved how romantic he was. Once she relieved Evander of the flowers, box of chocolate, and bottle of wine, he greeted Skye, who was prancing around, eagerly waiting to be noticed.

"I'll open the bottle of wine and take her out for a moment, if you aren't quite ready," he offered.

"Sure, that would be great."

After he opened the wine and poured it into wine glasses, she put the flowers into a vase of water. She thought he was going to take Skye out right after that, but he pulled Alyth into his arms and smiled. "Everyone in the pack thinks you need to be with me."

She smiled up at him. "I believe Nita thinks the same thing." She wondered if Lana had told him what she'd said about him at lunch, but she wasn't going to bring it up and he didn't. "Hmm, after dinner, can we go for another wolf run and see Shadow's puppies?"

He smiled. "Aye, I was counting on it."

"Great minds think alike." She kissed him and he kissed back, their tongues tangling with each other, and the passion ignited between them again. What was there about Evander that made her feel like *she* was in heat and wanted him in the worst way?

Their pheromones were doing a kick dance and she didn't want to let him go, but then she remembered the dinner. "Oh, I need to serve up the dinner." She didn't want to spoil it for him by ruining it and for him to think she was a bad cook.

He smiled. "All right. I'll take Skye out and be right back."

When Evander didn't come back in right away after she served the meal, she glanced out the window to see what he and Skye were doing. He was tossing the ball for Skye, and she was loving it, bouncing after it, and returning it to him. They were so cute, and she was glad he was playing with her. Then he said, "Come on, Skye, your momma's waiting for us."

Alyth set a couple of glasses of water on the table. Evander came in with Skye and set her leash on the brass hook, washed up, then joined Alyth at the dinner table.

"This is grand. You could teach our cook about this," he said after he'd eaten a few bites of his chicken.

Alyth laughed. "I just learned how to do it from a recipe I found on the internet last year. It's really good." She sipped some of her wine. "The wine is too."

He took another bite of the chicken. "The chicken is delicious."

"Thank you."

"Oh." He brought out his phone and she thought he heard a text message or something that she hadn't heard, and he needed to respond to. But he looked for something, and then handed her his phone.

With all twelve of her puppies nursing, Shadow was stretched out on her side on her bed resting. Evander was so sweet to share the picture of her with Alyth.

"Poor thing. And to think I probably put Skye through that also."

"If Magnus didn't give her pups, Dillon might have anyway."

Alyth lifted her wine glass. "I wonder how Cal would feel if the first time his dog mated with her, he was—"

"Shooting blanks?"

She laughed.

"That's why Cal agreed to three sessions. That's usually the way it is."

"But if she has puppies that were Dillon's on the first time that he had mated her—"

"He's a stud, what can I say."

She laughed again. She was thinking Evander was too.

After dinner, he was going to help clean up, but she said no to that. "I can get it later. Let's go for our run and I want to see Shadow and her pups. But let me change first." She didn't want to wear her fancier kilt that she was wearing at the shop today, and slipped into a pair of jeans, a long-sleeved shirt, and tennis shoes.

Then he drove her over to his place, and they went inside the cottage and did the same as before—stripped and shifted and headed out for a run along the beach. She saw four other wolves out running on the sandy shore this time and they greeted her. Heather and Lana, and a couple of wolves Alyth hadn't met, but she recognized them from their scents.

The other wolves took off and returned to the castle and Alyth and Evander had the beach to themselves again. When she looked up high on the hill, she could see that the wall walk and castle windows looked out on the beach. She hadn't paid attention to it before. Now she wondered if anyone was watching them!

They romped in the surf and playfought this time, then they finally raced each other back to the stairs to the castle walkway. At least this time, no one howled to end their play. She was eager to see Shadow and the puppies next and then call it a night. She was still tired from last night and not getting enough sleep. Still, she had to do this or all she would think about was missing out on seeing Shadow and her pups.

After they dressed at Evander's cottage and went to the kennel, Shadow had just left her puppies to relieve herself and soon came back inside and greeted them. She looked just as happy to see Alyth, and then they went in to check on her puppies. Some were sleeping in a bundle of six, and the others were trying to find their momma.

Oran greeted them in the whelping room. "Lana said you went for a run."

"Aye, Alyth wanted to see Shadow and her puppies after that."

Shadow came in and laid down on the floor and several of the puppies were vying for a teat.

"Everyone has been doing great tonight, while you were out," Oran told Evander. "My brothers and I are taking turns caring for them when you leave for the night."

"Okay, thanks."

Alyth was already sitting on the floor, the paper having been freshly cleaned. She stroked the sleeping puppies. "How many males and females?"

Evander joined her. "Half and half."

"Do you have buyers for them?"

"Half of them already. Once they're a little older, we'll take more photos of them, though we have posted them already for potential buyers on our kennel website," Evander said. "In the beginning, Ian hadn't wanted us to make a real business out of this, but it's become really profitable, and we can always use the extra money for the clan and for the upkeep of the castle."

"I love having a female, but sometimes I wonder if it wouldn't be easier—for breeding purposes—to have a male for stud services."

Oran agreed.

Evander stroked Shadow's head. "There is an advantage to it, if the dog makes champion, the better the income. The male can breed at any time. So aye, he could breed with twelve different females and end up making the same as the amount Shadow's litter will bring. No vet bills to have to pay out either."

"Still having lots of little puppies is pure joy," she said.

"I totally agree with you there," Evander said.

A couple of the pups raised their heads as if they realized the milk was nearby and they were hungry again. They began to struggle to get to momma. Alyth carried them over to Shadow and they latched onto her teats.

"You would totally spoil them," Oran said.

Evander chuckled. "She would."

She smiled. "I would."

7

That night, Evander took Alyth home and Skye was so excited to greet them, treating Evander just like he was part of her family now. He loved it. He loved her and he adored Alyth. After they had glasses of champagne, he wanted to stay overnight, but he didn't want to pressure Alyth if she wasn't ready for it. Even though his sister had told him how much Alyth really, really liked him.

She didn't seem to be ready to have him stay with her overnight yet as they finished their glasses and she washed them, then he dried them.

"I'm a little worried about..." she said.

He took her hands, and he pulled her into his embrace. "About what?"

"I keep thinking about the night that Skye got away, and she and Dillon joined each other on the island."

"Aye."

"I was sure I had shut my gate. But then why else would it have been open if I hadn't left it that way accidentally?"

Evander frowned at her, rubbing her shoulders. "You think someone might have been up to mischief?"

"Probably not. Maybe I didn't close the gate all the way, that it didn't catch, and then the wind blew it the rest of the way open."

"But you're worried there's more to it."

"Yeah. Just a little bit. I know this sounds crazy but, I saw a red Kia Picanto sitting at the bakery when that happened, but their store and mine weren't open yet and I didn't recognize the vehicle. It's not the owner's car. When I returned home with Skye, the car was gone. I only vaguely remembered it had been there when I had to chase down Skye. Until I saw it again the morning when I went to get groceries before work. It just made me feel uneasy. I returned to the house and had poor Nita come over early to dog sit before we opened the store, which I've never done. I had to get groceries, but I was worried about leaving Skye alone when I saw that red car again. After Nita showed up, I left the house and saw that the red car was gone."

"I've always gone by gut instinct until it's proven wrong. It's better to trust it and be more prepared if it turns out your instinct was right. We're wolves after all. And there's something to be said about that."

"Yeah, me too," Evander said, worrying that someone was targeting Alyth's deerhound.

"What are the chances that someone might be interested in grabbing Skye because she could be carrying puppies that are worth a lot of money?" she asked.

"Dog napping and selling off puppies can be a big business. Not only that, but Skye would be worth a lot of money too. Until they change the laws regarding pet theft, if the dog nappers get caught, they don't get more than a slap on the wrist for stealing someone's beloved pet." Evander let out his breath. He didn't want to tell Alyth what she should do, but he was afraid his suggestions might sound that way. "It's up to you, but for your own peace of mind, you have several options. We could take

Skye to the castle, to the kennel, where she would have her own room and after the final mating between her and Magnus, she won't be in heat either. But we would make sure that she is taken well care of."

"I want her at home like she has always been. I'm not sure she would like to be at a kennel for two months before her pups are born, and then for longer until they are old enough to find their forever homes. You know how deerhounds and wolfhounds are. They like to be with people. Though I guess she would love to be with the other dogs. But I think she would miss me too much, just like I would miss her."

Which he had figured. "The Irish wolfhounds all go to the castle to play with the kids and run around on the castle grounds too. So they aren't cooped up in the kennels all the time. Just mainly for sleeping at night. The rest of the time, they're with members of the wolf pack. Except, of course, in the case of dams like Shadow that just had her pups or dams in heat. Even then, we are with them lots during the day to make sure they're not feeling neglected. And of course, once Shadow's puppies are older, she'll be out with the whole pack, the members all playing with her puppies and cuddling them to give her a much-needed break and showing her as much attention also."

"Okay, that sounds good. Another option would be the two of you could stay at my cottage with me and then any time we're out running around together, someone will stay there with her. She would be at home and not at the kennel then, but you would have everyone from the wolf pack at her beck and call. No one would even entertain the thought of stealing her at the castle estate, if anyone has been trying to. And if they did, they would sorely regret it."

She gave him a small smile. "That could be a real inconvenience to you though if we stayed there with you."

"Not at all. I would love it if you and Skye stayed with me, and we have enough people in the pack who would be happy to help. Or the other option could be that I stay with the two of you at night at your place and take turns taking her outside to relieve herself in the evenings because if she's carrying puppies, she'll feel the urge to go outside more frequently as her due date grows closer."

"Again, that's an inconvenience to you if you have to stay with me and what if you're needed at the kennels?"

"Everything will be covered."

She let out her breath. "And if I'm wrong that anything is going on?"

"Then it's still better to be safe than sorry. If we have more of us watching out for her, she's not going to go missing. We can do whatever you feel most comfortable doing. Or we can even change things up. You can stay with me some nights and days when your store is closed. We'll have fun taking her for walks on the estate, and we can stay at your place on the other nights so that you can have your normal routine then. We can set up a birthing box at my place too just in case she's there when she has her pups. If we go out on a dinner date, we'll have a couple of people watch her. I can stay with you tonight, if you would like."

She smiled brightly at him. "That was your plan all along."

He laughed and kissed her. "I think that was *your* plan all along."

She chuckled. "Okay, that works for me, but you probably don't have anything with you—"

"I'll be right back. That's what is nice about you being located so close to the estate. But it only would take someone a couple of minutes to snatch a dog and tear off, so it would be best if I'm actually here."

"All right. If you change your mind about all this, don't hesitate to tell me. I don't want to put you out."

"It's not happening. You would have a whole bunch of bachelor males knocking down your door to take my place." Then he kissed her again. "I'll be back in a jiffy."

"Thanks."

"You're so welcome. And thank you for letting me help out." Then he left her while she locked the door. He realized then that was probably why she had begun locking her gate. He wished she'd told him right away about her concerns because the pack would help her out and he didn't want her worrying about it. He called Ian on the way to his cottage, furious that he hadn't caught the driver of the red car. "Hey, it's Evander. I'm on my way to pack a few things at my cottage and stay with Alyth."

"Sounds like things are moving right along between the two of you."

"It's not exactly what you think. There's a red car that has been randomly showing up across the street from Alyth's place and she's not sure she actually opened the gate the morning that Skye ran off and got together with Dillon."

"She's worried about a possible case of dog napping?" Ian asked, sounding concerned.

"Aye. Anyone might have been following Cal while he made his trips to breed his dog with Alyth's and then would know Skye could be carrying pups soon."

"We'll have some of our men check around for the vehicle and learn what's going on."

"Thanks, Ian. I'm sure that will help make Alyth feel better."

"For sure. We're here for her."

"Thanks." Evander told Ian their plan that he would stay at her place and his, taking the dog with them and having someone watch Skye whenever he and Alyth went out together. He couldn't believe that someone could be targeting her dog, and he would do everything to make sure that Skye and Alyth stayed safe. He knew Ian would task someone to look into it right away. Then they ended the call.

Evander parked at his cottage and hurried inside to pack up his things so he could spend the night with Alyth. He couldn't believe how much their dogs had brought them together. And he was damn glad for it.

He soon returned to her place, glanced in the direction of the closed bakery shop—no red car—grabbed his bag from his car, then knocked at her front door. Skye didn't even bark, as if she knew it was him. She probably did. She would have recognized the sound of his car engine. Though Skye, being a deerhound, might not have barked anyway.

Alyth hurried to the door and opened it and gave Evander a big hug. "Thanks for staying with me. I feel so much better about this."

Feeling great about her welcome, Evander hugged her back and kissed her, then shut and locked the door behind him. He told her what Ian was going to do about looking for the red car.

"Oh, thanks so much. If it's nothing, that will be great. At least I can put the concern behind me."

"Exactly. Do you want me to take Skye out one last time?" Evander asked.

"Yeah, sure, thanks. I'm going to jump in the shower. I'll take your bag into the bedroom."

He smiled. "Your bedroom or a guest room or the couch in the—"

"My room."

"Yes!" He was thrilled!

She laughed.

He attached Skye's leash to her pink, rhinestone collar. "Ready to go out?"

Skye wagged her tail like crazy.

Alyth smiled, grabbed Evander's bag, and hauled it into the master bedroom.

ALYTH HATED that someone might even be considering trying to steal her dog, but she was really glad Evander was staying with her and in *her* bedroom! She couldn't wait. She took her shower, dried off, and dressed in a pair of pajama shorts and a shirt, but when she left the bathroom, she realized Evander wasn't in the bedroom yet. She couldn't believe it was taking that long for Skye to finish her business outside. Poor Evander.

Alyth threw on a robe and slippers and peeked out the window to the backyard. The porchlight was on outside, illuminating a good portion of the yard except for the fence in the back and the side yards. She expected to see Evander and Skye playing with the ball maybe, though she would be surprised because it was time for bed, and she was well past ready for him to join her.

Neither Skye nor Evander were in the main part of the yard. Trying not to panic, she couldn't stop her heart from pounding like crazy. She went to the back door, opened it, and ran outside to the gate at the side of the property. Evander's clothes were lying on the grass next to the gate. Oh, no!

She was certain Evander wouldn't have left the yard as a wolf unless Skye had run away. She checked the lock on the gate and her worst fears were realized. The lock on the gate had been cut. Immediately, she raced back inside the house and called Ian MacNeill, since he was going to help her with this situation if it was a case of attempted dog napping.

"Hi, it's Alyth. Evander took Skye out into the backyard, but they've run off. He's running as a wolf, and the lock to the gate had been cut."

"I'm calling up the troops and on my way."

"I'm going after them as a wolf," she said, kicking off her slippers, yanking off her robe, pulling off her pajama top, and then her shorts in the living room. "I'm off to find them." She locked the back door. She wasn't hanging around here when she might be able to help Evander catch Skye.

"All right. We're on our way over there." Then Ian ended the call.

She was glad he hadn't suggested that she stay at the house because she had no intention of doing it. She had to find Skye and Evander. If they were in trouble, she wanted to help them out.

She set her phone down on the kitchen table. Then she shifted into her wolf and dove through the wolf door and followed the scents of both Evander and Skye. She glanced in the direction of the bakery, looking to see if the red car was there, but not really expecting it to be. If they had been waiting for Skye, then when she was gone, they would have gone after her. If they had seen Skye tear off, what would they have thought of a wolf chasing after her?

They probably would assume Evander was a German shepherd though. She couldn't understand how Skye would have gotten away from Evander when he had her on her leash. Then again, when she'd watched them before, Evander had let go of the leash to give her a little freedom. He must have done that before he realized the gate was open. Since it was around the side of the house, he couldn't see that it was open unless he went around the corner of the building.

She stopped for a moment and lifted her chin and howled, hoping Evander would howl back to let her know they were okay.

Then she heard Evander howl from the direction of the

MacNeill castle. Not there again! Was Skye trying to see Dillon? But Skye didn't break the lock to the gate.

Alyth ran full out to join Evander, hoping he'd gotten hold of Skye's leash. Skye could give any wolf a run for the money with her long legs.

Then a van pulled up on the road she was crossing to reach the MacNeill estate, scaring her. She didn't want anyone to see her. But then Ian got out of the passenger's side of the vehicle and called to her. "Alyth!"

She turned her head to look at him, panting, wanting to keep going to Evander's aid.

"Evander's at the cottage with Skye. Jump in. We'll take you there."

She glanced in the direction of the woods, then turned and headed for the van. If it hadn't been that she knew who he was, she would have kept running, worried he was a dog napper and aiming to take *her* hostage.

"I'm so sorry about this," Ian said, as he closed the door to the van, and she sat on one of the bench seats. He sat up front with the driver, his brother, Duncan. "We'll get whoever this is."

She realized she'd smelled a man's scent by her gate before. The first time, it really hadn't registered that an unfamiliar male scent had been by it when the gate had been left open. But now that the lock had been cut, she had smelled the same scent.

Duncan parked the van at Evander's cottage. "We'll drive you, Evander, and Skye back to your place if you want. You can go in and check with Evander and decide what the two of you want to do."

Ian opened the door for her, and she woofed at them, then jumped out of the van and ran for the cottage. She hoped the wolf door was unlocked because she was running into Evander's cottage to see him and Skye at breakneck speed. Before she could reach his door, he pulled it open, standing there in the nude, the most beautiful specimen of a man as before. He smiled at her, and she rushed past him to find Skye drinking water from a large dog dish.

She stood there watching her, relief washing over her, panting, realizing she needed some water too.

"I take it our chariot awaits," Evander said, shutting the door. "I'll get dressed."

She shifted. "Maybe we should stay here the night."

Dressed in his boxer briefs, he came over to hug her. "All right. I'll tell them we're staying here. But they'll be looking for the culprits too."

"Did you smell the man's scent by the gate? I had smelled it before."

"Yeah." Then he called Ian on his landline since he'd left his cell phone at her house, just like she had. "Hey, we're staying here for the night." Evander glanced at Alyth. "Did you lock up your house?"

"Yes, not the wolf door though."

"Do you want to return there for some clothes or other personal things?"

She shook her head.

"Okay, we're good. Thanks." He glanced at Skye. "Yeah, I'll make a bed for Skye also." Then he hung up the phone.

"It's a good thing you have a landline still," she said, wrapping a blanket from the couch around her.

He pulled a box out of a room. "Yeah, I never thought I would need it because I'd left my cell phone at a beautiful she-wolf's place."

"Or that you would need to continually chase after a wild, out-of-control deerhound."

He smiled and added some newspapers to the box and left it near the kitchen. "It's too early for her to be having any puppies, but just in case she feels like nesting."

While he was taking care of Skye, Alyth went into the kitchen to get a glass of water. "So what happened exactly? I saw where the lock was broken."

"Yeah. Skye kept looking for a spot to relieve herself in the yard. Sometimes the dogs don't care to go on a leash, and since she'd been fine before with me letting go of her leash, especially since I knew the gate was locked, I let her go."

"Like you did when you were playing fetch with her."

"Aye and everything was fine. Except she must have heard the gate open about the same time I heard a slight squeak. Being in her dog form, she bounded off to check it out. I raced after her but too late. Then it took me a couple of minutes to strip and shift and race after her. She's damn fast."

"I know. Did you see the red car?"

"No, just Skye heading in the direction of the MacNeill estate."

"To meet up with Dillon."

"You have to admit the two of them have a special connection between them."

Alyth groaned. "I don't want to hear it. Do you have something for me to wear to bed?"

"A long T-shirt or a pair of sweats?"

They walked into his bedroom, and he began pulling clothes out of a drawer that she might like to wear.

"The long T-shirt with the Irish wolfhounds on it. For promoting the pups, right?"

"Aye." He handed it to her, and she handed the blanket to him, then pulled the shirt over her head. "We wear them whenever we have a new litter."

"Wow, that's such a cool idea." She pulled the covers aside. "Does it matter which side of the bed that I sleep on?"

"Either is fine with me. I'm so sorry about letting go of Skye's leash. If I hadn't—"

"We wouldn't be sleeping in your bed instead of mine." She kissed him and he pulled her into his embrace and kissed her back. "No harm done and thanks so much for going after her like you did. Now we know there's someone who is really trying to grab Skye. At least I believe so. There's nothing else anyone could want in my yard or at the house, I wouldn't think."

"Agreed." Evander climbed onto the other side of the bed, but then they gravitated toward each other.

Even though he had set up the box for Skye near the kitchen, she joined them in the bedroom and laid down next to Evander's side of the bed, which both surprised and amused her.

"Traitor," Alyth said, glad Skye liked Evander so much.

"She's all into guys right now," Evander said, chuckling.

Alyth kissed him on the mouth. "Yeah, like I am into you right now."

"I feel totally the same way about you."

Then he gently took hold of her face and began kissing her. With just a kiss and a warm embrace, he recharged her energy. All thoughts of dog nappers and runaway dogs immediately faded from her mind. His kisses were powerful and pleasurable, and she loved kissing him. Their pheromones had immediately kickstarted and she felt heady from the scents swirling around them. His mouth was hot, and he seemed just as needy as her as he stroked her tongue with delicious intensity.

His hand moved over her breast, caressing, molding to it, the T-shirt fabric soft against her skin. Her nipples were already perked and reveling in his touch. She breathed in his rich scent, the grass and heather he'd run through as a wolf still making him as fragrant as the wild out of doors, his wolf and man all combined. She smelled of grass and heather too.

She listened to his heart—and hers—beating rapidly. His hands on her body were tender and aroused her as she ran her hands over the planes of his torso. His hard muscles were divine, and he flexed them a little, making her laugh. He was setting her blood aflame, but he was fun to be with too. He drew in a breath and growled a little while she moved her hand over his heated skin, and she smiled.

Skye started to snore and both Alyth and Evander chuckled. Evander slid his mouth over Alyth's neck and kissed her throat. She had dreamt of being with him like this, of kissing him in bed, of making unconsummated love with him, of snuggling with him the rest of the night.

He pulled up the long T-shirt she was wearing and tossed it aside. She reached down and slid his boxer briefs off him and tossed them also. He was already fully aroused. Impressive. *Really* impressive. She ran her hand over his erection, and it throbbed in her hand. *Hmm. Glorious.*

He drank her in completely before he began kissing her again, her mouth first, then her ear, nibbling on the lobe for a moment, sending a thrill cascading through her. But when he found her aroused nubbin and began stroking, she gasped with pleasure. He definitely had the right moves.

His gaze on hers was hot as he cast her a knowing smile and licked her lips. He paused only a moment from stroking her while he was kissing her, and she was dying for him to keep going. But then he was back to rubbing her. And she was ecstatic. Every stroke pushed her further. She was slowly rising to the top, feeling the climax coming, wanting, no...needing desperately for it to succeed. Evander was the wolf to make it happen, she knew.

As if he sensed it, maybe smelled that she was close to coming, he began stroking her faster. She was breathing harder, her pulse quickening, and she could just feel the end. Then it hit her, and she felt the escalation and the end all at once, and she cried out his name. "Evander! Ohmigod, you are beautiful. You are so...talented."

His gaze locked onto hers, he chuckled.

But now it was his turn to come, and she reached down to grasp his length and began to stroke him. He sucked in his breath and released, then began to kiss her again. He tasted so good, and she couldn't help but drink him in. Fiery passion consumed them as he reached down and placed his hand over her hand and helped her stroke him faster.

She smiled and whispered, "In a wee bit of a hurry?"

"Oh, God, aye."

She chuckled and stroked him faster, holding him firmer to see how he reacted to that, and he groaned with pleasure. She loved it and he seemed to also.

Then he came and she kept going until she had milked him completely. He pulled her into his arms and just hugged the breath from her. "Man, oh, man. You are such a wolf."

"You are too," she said.

He kissed her deeply, then said, "Shower time?"

"Hmm, absolutely."

And of course, Skye had to get up and went with them to the bathroom, sitting down while they stepped into the shower and enjoyed each other. Whereupon Skye finally fell asleep beside the shower.

8

A lyth and Evander snuggled together. She was upset about the business with worrying if someone was going to steal Skye, but she was glad she and Evander were staying together now. She knew that after the situation was resolved with the dog napper, she didn't want this to end with Evander.

In the morning, she woke with a start after such a nice time with Evander in bed. "Ohmigod. It's...it's late. I've got to go!"

"We've got time. Julia dropped off some clothes for you and I'm taking you to have breakfast up at the castle."

As soon as she realized Skye wasn't greeting her, Alyth frowned. "Where's Skye?"

"I took her out and then I walked her up to the castle. She was ready to spend some time with just our dams. They're keeping her company. I figured you needed to sleep. And then I rejoined you in bed." He hurried to dress.

"I'm glad you came back to bed."

He smiled. "Of course. I didn't want you to wake up alone."

"I would have worried Skye had gone for a run again and you

were out chasing her down." Alyth dressed, and then they went outside and walked to the castle walls. She was amazed at how massive the outer walls were, ten feet wide, she thought, and she had no idea how tall they were. The sun had risen, and Evander was right. She had the time to enjoy eating breakfast at the castle with the rest of the pack members. This would be fun. Maybe she would learn something about what had happened about the red car.

"I had a great night, by the way," she said to Evander, clasping his hand.

"Oh, I agree. I'm already to do it again tonight."

She laughed. "Yeah, me too."

Then they greeted others in the great hall, and everyone was eager to see her. Julia came over to give her a hug.

"Thanks so much, Julia, for loaning me some clothes," Alyth said, hugging her back.

"You're so welcome. We're about the same size. We always help out when someone needs clothing in a situation like yours," Julia said.

"Well, I appreciate it."

"We'll sit over here," Evander said.

"Sure."

"Oh, thanks so much for selling so many of my books. It's way beyond my expectations," Julia said.

"It's been great fun," Alyth said. Then she and Evander sat next to Lana.

"Did you hear about the dog napper who tried to steal a Scottish deerhound in Edinburgh?" Lana asked. "I believe right now, that's all any of us are thinking about. We adore Skye. She's such a sweetheart and she has had a great time with our females."

"And probably wants to be with the males," Alyth said, knowing her dog after this experience.

"Aye, of course. But it's totally a dog condition. It's a good thing us wolves aren't wired in that way," Lana said.

"I agree. Whose dog was nearly stolen? Was she or he returned? Are the dog and owner okay?" Alyth asked.

"Aye. The owner startled the would-be thief and hit him with a walking stick when he broke into her home. Unfortunately, she wasn't able to incapacitate him, and he managed to get away. She called the police right away. Since the dog is a Scottish deerhound, it made me think of yours," Lana said, as breakfast of eggs, biscuits, and ham was served.

"No. Who was the owner?"

"Rebecca Johnson. She's—"

"American. Her dam is Skye's mother. Rebecca has only the one deerhound and she lives in Edinburgh." Alyth was horrified to learn of it.

"Oh, no. Well, the dog is fine. So is Rebecca," Lana said.

"Can I borrow your phone? Mine's back at my house," Alyth said, anxious to learn how her friend was faring.

"My phone also," Evander said. "Or I would loan you mine."

"Yeah, sure." Lana handed her phone to Alyth.

She called Rebecca then, sorry to be rude to Lana and Evander at the dining table, but she knew how upset her friend had to be over this. "Hi, Rebecca, are you okay?"

"Alyth? You're calling from someone else's phone?"

"Yeah. Skye ran off again and I chased after"—she glanced at Evander—"her, but Evander Cameron was running as a wolf to catch her. So neither of us have our phones on us. But Evander's sister, Lana, was telling me about Princess being stolen. Your Princess. And the thing is it appears someone might be trying to steal Skye too."

"No." Rebecca sounded astounded that it had happened to her also.

"Aye."

"Tell Rebecca she can stay here with the MacNeill Clan if she would like with her dog, if she's a wolf too," Evander said. "She would be welcome."

Alyth said, "You have an offer to stay at Argent Castle to keep you and Princess safe until all the culprits are caught. I heard you knocked out one of the dog nappers."

"I sure did, but not hard enough so that the police could catch him."

"I'm just glad he didn't hurt you or Princess."

"I'm so glad also. There could be others working with him. I'm not sure about staying at the MacNeill castle though. I don't like to impose on others that I don't really know."

"They're a wolf pack. You'll love them. They'll love you. And you can keep Princess here with you and she'll be safe."

"A castle, eh?"

"Yeah. Don't tell me you've stayed at one before."

Rebecca didn't say anything for a moment. "Okay, but I need to talk to whoever owns the castle first to make sure it's really all right."

"They're the pack leaders, clan leaders, and own the castle." Alyth told Julia what had happened.

"Let me talk to her." Julia took Lana's phone from Alyth. "Hi, I'm Julia MacNeill, pack leader and clan leader of the MacNeill pack, along with my mate, Ian. We would be happy to have you and Princess come stay with us." She smiled at Alyth. "We would be honored, and we all would feel better about it if we knew you and Princess were safe. We also have plenty of room here for guests and Princess can stay with you, and you can run as a wolf whenever you like." She paused. "All right. We'll see you tomorrow morning." Julia handed the phone back to Alyth.

"Hey, Rebecca, I'm so glad you're going to stay with the MacNeills for a while. I'll come and see you, run as a wolf with you too. And of course let Princess and Skye see each other. I'm sure it will be a happy reunion."

"Absolutely. See you soon. Thanks for calling and checking up on me. And thanks for helping me out with this. I can't wait to meet Evander too, since you still haven't taken a photo of him to share with me."

Alyth laughed. "Okay, see you." Then she felt a lot better that Rebecca and Princess would be here and safe and handed the phone to Lana. "Thanks so much. Oh, shoot, I need to eat breakfast quickly so I can get to the shop and open it."

"What do you want to do about Skye?" Lana asked. "Can you leave her here with us? I mean, at the castle? I have to go to Heather's pie shop to bake."

"I think that might be a good idea. If I'm busy at the shop, I might not notice anyone trying to break into the house to grab Skye."

"I'll bring her over to your home and then stay there for the night, or we can come back here and stay the night," Evander said.

"Sure. Either works for me." She hurried to eat her breakfast and then she thanked everyone, said her goodbyes, and checked on Skye, who was thrilled to see her. Then she felt bad that she was leaving her here. But if she didn't, she worried that she might lose her for good. Her and the puppies.

Then Oran drove Alyth and Evander back to her place so Evander could pick up his car. Evander saw Alyth to her house, and she kissed him goodbye. Their lips lingered and they both smiled.

"Seriously, it's hard for me to let go of you," Evander said.

Smiling, Oran was shaking his head as he watched them from his car.

"I know. I feel the same way about you."

"Okay, I'm off to the castle before I get fired."

"And before Nita quits on me for always being late to work once you and I started dating."

He laughed. "I know." Then he said he'd see her later, which she was glad for, and he left in his car, following Oran out of her driveway.

She showered, dressed in her own clothes, and hurried into the store. Nita was already there, opening the store.

"So how are things progressing with you and Evander?"

"Great."

Nita was sure to think that Alyth had been home last night because her car and Evander's had been at the house.

"But we had other troubles last night. Skye ran off, but Evander caught up to her as a wolf. The problem is that someone cut the lock to the gate," Alyth said.

"Oh, no. To steal Skye?"

"We think so."

"So the morning the gate was open when Skye got away the first time wasn't your fault?" Nita asked.

"I don't think so. I didn't think so back then, and I believe now someone tried to steal her that time too. So the MacNeills are keeping her at the castle for the time being."

"You don't have any more dates breeding Magnus to Skye, do you?"

"No. We're done, which I'm glad for, especially with all the trouble I'm having keeping Skye away from other dogs. We'll decide where we're going to stay after this." Alyth figured Nita would realize what was going on between her and Evander before long. "We stayed at Evander's cottage last night."

"Whoa."

Alyth smiled. "Yeah, things are moving right along." She told her about Skye's mother and how someone tried to steal her at her home in Edinburgh. "So Rebecca and her dam, Princess, is staying at the MacNeill's castle too."

"Oh, that's just awful. I'm glad she knocked the guy on the head but it's too bad he got away, and he wasn't arrested."

"I agree. Though he might think twice about trying to steal another dog."

"I'm glad the MacNeill wolf pack will take them both in. Will Skye get to see her momma then?" Nita asked, restocking one of the shelves with gift teas from Scotland.

"Aye. I'm sure they'll be thrilled to see each other again, except now Skye is all grown up and possibly full of puppies." Alyth added price tags to some new green plush Nellies (Loch Ness monsters that were the cutest), shaggy Highland plush cows, plush West Highland and Scottish terriers, and teddy bears with plaid vests.

"All the new merchandise is so cute," Nita said, casting a glance at the shelves and a baby pram that was filled with the stuffed toys. "And you know, just perfect for little ones when they arrive."

Alyth laughed. "Who needs little ones when the adults love them just as much!"

Then they got busy with orders and sales and early that evening, Evander turned up with Skye. Alyth was glad he was so considerate of her feelings and brought Skye with him.

Nita waved at them, and then said, "See you tomorrow."

"Night, Nita," Evander and Alyth said.

"I'll make Cullen skink for dinner if that appeals," Alyth said to Evander, giving him a big hug.

"I'll help you make it," Evander said.

"Yeah, that would be great." Alyth gave Skye a big hug next. She was so glad to see her dog again. "So are you full of puppies now?" She had wondered that every day now, ever since she had bred her to Magnus and after Skye had been with Dillon.

Skye just wagged her tail.

"I take that as an aye," Alyth said.

Evander said, "One way or another, I'm sure she is."

Alyth wanted to groan. When she thought of Magnus's pups growing in Skye's belly, she was excited. Dillon's? She was still afraid she might not find homes for them all, and she would have to pay the stud feed to Cal.

Then she and Evander began fixing dinner. He started boiling a large potato.

She combined the milk, parsley stalks, bay leaf, and finnan haddie, or smoked haddock, into a saucepan while he finely chopped up parsley leaves. After the mixture simmered, Evander dished out the haddock and she strained the herbs out of the milk. He chopped up the onion and she added butter and onion and cooked them while he mashed the potatoes.

She loved that they could complement each other like this when they were cooking. Then they added all the ingredients together except for the haddock and cooked it until it was thickened. They broke up the haddock into bite size pieces, continually bumping into each other and chuckling and stirred them gently into the soup.

He added the chopped parsley and once the meat was warm, he sprinkled a little salt and pepper and more parsley on top.

She was getting the bread warmed up. A nice crusty loaf. And then she served it while he ladled out the soup.

"This looks and smells delicious," she said.

"Yeah, that was fun making it together too. What would you like to drink?" He glanced in her pantry. "How about this? A glass of Lond Cru Chardonnay?"

"Perfect. It's got kind of a nutty, citrusy flavor, perfect to go with the Cullen skink."

"That sounds like a great pairing." He glanced at Skye. She was sitting at the door, wanting to go out again. As soon as he caught her eye, she wagged her tail vigorously. "It's not good timing, Skye. You're not just looking for a daddy dog, are you?"

"She better not be." Alyth was past ready for her to be out of heat.

"I'm afraid she could be interested in the male persuasion for a couple more weeks." He hooked Skye's leash up to her collar.

"I'll check to make sure the gate is locked!"

"Good idea, but I'm not letting go of her leash this time or any other time."

"I wouldn't either." Alyth went out first and found the gate locked. "Somebody changed out the lock on the gate."

"Yeah, but it's locked on the inside now, right?"

"Aye."

"One of wolf pack members would have done it. There were some keys on the island counter. Maybe they're the keys to the lock unless they're for something else."

"Oh, that must be what those are for. I wondered. They weren't mine." Then she frowned. "They came into the house?"

"Through the wolf door probably to leave the keys off for you last night and also to make sure no one had slipped into the house."

"Oh, true. I hadn't locked the wolf door. And now that you mention it, I do smell a male wolf's scent I hadn't noticed before."

"Yeah, that's Oran's scent." They watched and waited for Skye to find her spot of grass to relieve herself and then they returned to the house. Evander unhooked Skye's leash and he and Alyth sat down to eat.

"So what do you want to do after dinner?" Evander asked.

"Let's go to your place tonight after we finish up here. I don't want to feel that we can't safely stay at my place, but I believe for now staying at your place is the right thing to do."

"Okay, and we can go for a wolf run, see a movie, and there will be others in the pack who will be observing things. Also, just to let you know, they're watching out for us here while we're at the house. But I thought it would be nice to go for a wolf run."

"That's great that we have some additional support while we're here."

"You better believe it. They are watching for that car if it should show up or anything else that seems out of the ordinary. Even if we don't catch them right away, the dog thief might decide it's too much of a risk to go after her any further."

"I didn't see anyone observing my house or shop."

"Exactly. And you won't. Just like any potential dog thieves won't either."

"That's great news."

Once they finished their delicious soup, they cleaned up the kitchen and Alyth packed clothes, including the ones she'd borrowed from Julia, and they took Skye with them to Evander's cottage.

The place was a really big, one-story stone house, but it was sprawling, with four bedrooms and three baths. It was a short distance to the castle and had a big walled in yard, the dike built out of ancient stones littered on the land, covered with moss. He didn't have a garden or anything, just a big yard with a couple of oak trees. She guessed the large yard was for exercising any of the dogs but also for keeping them from running off. The wall was five-six feet tall, standing a couple of inches taller than Alyth.

"They recommend that we have at least a five-foot wall for Irish wolfhounds, but we added a little more height to make sure."

"Especially when runaway dams in heat are on the loose. I love the ancient stone wall. So Dillon wasn't in your yard when he ran off and met up with Skye."

"No. He was at the kennels, and he was loose in there, not in his room. As soon as I opened the kennel door, he raced past me. Of course at the time, I hadn't realized he was looking for a lassie to mate."

Smiling, Alyth shook her head. "Have you heard anything from the guys who are looking into the situation with the potential dog thief?"

"No. They'll let us know right away when they learn of anything."

She sighed. "I guess we just need to wait and see, but the suspense is killing me."

"I know. Me too. I want it resolved."

"I guess you've never had that trouble before with your dogs."

"No. They're too well protected with a whole wolf pack here and with being at the castle most of the time. That's about the best fortification you could have."

She nodded, then they stripped off their clothes to go for a wolf run. Skye was watching them, and Alyth knew she wanted to go with them, but she wasn't going *anywhere* until she was done hunting down stud dogs for herself!

Then Alyth shifted while Evander shut the bedroom door so Skye couldn't run after them through the wolf door.

Then he shifted and they ran together toward the wolf door to have some wolf fun and for the moment, not think about dog nappers. But then she wondered if the dog nappers had gone after any of the other dams that Magnus had serviced, either recently or in the past. She needed to ask him. But not while she was enjoying the night with Evander.

They played with each other all the way down the castle steps to the beach, chasing each other, hunting, nipping, and tackling each other, having great fun. She loved this with him and could enjoy doing it with him every evening after dinner. Mornings too, if they got up early enough. They splashed through the cold water and tackled each other there, up on their hind legs, nipping and biting each other, having the time of their lives.

Then she sat down on the beach, and he joined her, nuzzling her cheek and looking at the nighttime sky, flashes of lightning lighting up the dark clouds hiding most of the moon. The three-quarter moon glowed against part of the dark clouds as if trying to make its presence known. The night was beautiful while the approaching storm was coming nearer while she sat with Evander and watched it, making it all the more pleasurable.

But then the rain started coming down, and he nudged at her to go. She was ready, though she had loved every moment of the time she'd spent with him while they were wolves. They took off across the sandy, rocky beach until they reached the steps leading up the steep hill. He let her go up the stairs first, but he was right behind her. She could feel his gentle nips at her tail as she held it straight out behind her as if telling her to hurry up because he was getting too wet, and she wanted to laugh.

Once they got to the top of the stairs, they headed along the path in the direction of the cottage. Their double fur coats as wolves kept their bodies dry, the softer undercoat warm against their bodies and the coarser outer coat with guard hairs repelling the rain. When they finally reached the covered deck of the cottage, the rain was coming down in a deluge, lightning lighting up the sky, thunder shaking the earth around them. She shook off the excess water from her coat. And got Evander even wetter. Before he could instinctively shake off his wolf's coat and get her back, she dashed in through the wolf door.

He howled on the deck, sounding amused that he had missed the opportunity to get her wet...or wetter. She howled indoors and Skye barked. Skye normally didn't bark when Alyth returned home, but she figured the howling had made her want to join in on the fun.

Alyth raced straight to the bedroom, shifted, and opened the door. Skye wagged her tail and nuzzled Alyth affectionately. Thankfully, Alyth had taught her not to jump in greeting. If she hadn't, Skye would have knocked her down.

Evander was right behind Alyth, shifting, petting Skye, then scooping Alyth up and carrying her into the bathroom. He kissed her forehead. "Ready for a hot shower?"

Skye followed them into the bathroom and sat down at Evander's feet as if he had been talking to her.

"With you? Absolutely. Skye loves baths so she's ready too."

He laughed. "We'll give her a bath some other time."

Now this was a new experience for Alyth. They were both naked, a little wet, and both chilled, so this was a perfect end to the night. "Tomorrow," she said as they got into the shower and began soaping each other, "I would like to see Rebecca and have Skye reunited with her momma."

"Absolutely. She said she was coming in the morning so we could have breakfast with them."

"Yeah, that would work. And then I'll head over to work, and Skye can stay at the castle with Princess?"

"Aye. I'll drive you to work and then head back to check on all the dogs."

"That won't be a problem, will it? I mean taking off to return me home."

"Not at all. You live so close, it's not a problem. Even if you lived farther away, it wouldn't be a problem."

They finished washing each other, and then dried off. Skye was eagerly waiting for them to pay attention to her. They both chuckled and she wagged her tail vigorously. After they both hugged her, they headed to bed. Skye hurried after them. She was always like a shadow when she was around Alyth. Sometimes, Alyth wished that she would just relax and not jump up every time she moved, but when Skye hadn't stayed with her, Alyth sure missed having her around her.

Then Alyth and Evander climbed into bed to finish the night in the most pleasurable way. She loved making love to him in this way, but she was sure the time would come when they would go all the way. As wolves, they didn't wait for a long time to decide such a thing. A few weeks. A couple of months, normally no more than three. It was just instinctual for them to know which wolf was right for them. It was a chemical, emotional, and biological connection. Their pheromones sang to each other when she'd never felt the chemistry between her and another wolf. They would have their ups and downs as all couples would, but she was certain he was the one for her.

When they began loving on each other, every touch brought her raw and earthy pleasure. She felt a loss of control and the need soul deep to have him all the way.

The way he kissed her was like she was the sweetest nectarine he'd ever tasted. The manner in which he breathed her in was as if he couldn't get enough of her scent, to memorize it, to savor it. His touching her from her face to her mons with heated passion from gentle to needy and everything in between made her crave him even more. He was such a hot prospect from his wolf's to his man's physique, to the way he smiled and kissed and hugged her. She was so glad to have him in her life, fulfilling her most passionate wishes.

She kissed his naked chest and took a deep breath of his fine spicy scent and all maleness. He likewise nuzzled the back of her ear that gave her exquisite chills up her spine. "Hmm," she said, and licked his nipple and then the other.

He groaned.

She smiled and kissed his mouth, his hands on her shoulders heating her to the core as his tongue skillfully stroked hers. He was both tender and hot and passionate. She was so wet for him. Her erect nipples rubbed against his hard chest, and she felt glorious. Then he kissed her belly and moved his fingers to the place between her legs that was pleading for his touch.

He began to stroke her, and she gave in to his intense touch, a flood of sensation rushing through her. When she was like this with him, she felt a wildness that she'd never felt for any other man. He was her wolf for sure.

Lightning flashed outside and a crack of thunder crashed outside.

"That's the power of our love," he whispered, but he wasn't stopping and continued to stroke her, making her tense, tingly, so, so needy.

"Keep going," she said in hushed desperation.

"Aye, lass." And he continued to touch her and elicit moans and groans from her, kissing her mouth at intervals until she couldn't last.

She cried out with orgasm. "Ohmigod, you are a dream in the flesh."

"You are so too."

She rolled him over onto his back and ran her hand over his chest, teasing his nipples, making them stand to attention. He was tensing, smiling, enjoying what she was doing to him she could tell. She leaned over and kissed and licked one, and then the other. His arousal was standing completely erect. But she wasn't ready to go that far yet. She licked a trail down to his navel and kissed it.

His erection jumped and he just groaned. "You're torturing me."

"I haven't even begun," she whispered against his ear and then she began to stroke him because she felt she had delayed giving him the ultimate pleasure long enough. She loved making him feel good. It made her happy.

She felt him tensing and she slowed her strokes, but then he groaned again. "You're killing me."

She chuckled and began stroking him faster again. She loved feeling the hardness of his erection, the way he reacted to her firm hand on him until he practically held his breath, his heart beating hard, and he erupted in a glorious way.

They kissed and then she hopped off the bed. "Shower now?"

"You bet." And he moved off the bed and swept her up in his arms and carried her into the bathroom. Skye was up for the adventure too. He turned on the shower and then they stepped inside and shut the door.

She loved that he was a dog person like her, a wolf who knew what he wanted just like she did, that he was so good to both her and her dog. She hadn't had anyone like that in her life since her parents had passed away. Being with him was both comforting and refreshing and made her feel like part of a family again.

Skye curled up beside the shower stall and they both laughed and began to soap each other up. "We'll have to play with her in the water tomorrow, give her a bath."

"After work, that will be first thing on the agenda."

"I'll hold you to it." That was another reason she felt he was so right for her. He got an at-home groomer at Skye's beck and call too.

"That is the easy part. Cleaning all her puppies? Now that will be an adventure."

She hadn't even thought about that part!

9

"Hmm, you are too enticing to give up for even a moment," Evander said to Alyth early the next morning. "You captured my heart from the moment I'd laid eyes on you. And I don't even want to leave you alone for a whole day. If I can and you are okay with it, I'll stop by the shop and have lunch with you."

"I feel the same thing about you. And aye, that would be great. Okay, let's go to the castle and meet up with Rebecca and Princess and have breakfast with them. Then I need to get to work, and you do too."

They finally got out of bed, both reluctant to leave each other. They kissed, sighed, and then they dressed and went up to the castle with Skye. The deerhound was so thrilled to go with them for a walk, though Evander held tightly onto her leash so she wouldn't get away from them. But she was too eager to go to the castle where all the male doggies were and wasn't interested in running off to anywhere else.

"How long will she be receptive to male dogs?" Alyth asked, sounding exasperated.

Evander leaned over and kissed her. "About five more days. But it can be longer."

Alyth sighed. "Okay, about five more days of this craziness. I'm going to think positively about this."

He laughed. "Aye."

Then they arrived at the castle and once they walked inside, they met up with Rebecca and Princess. Alyth hugged her friend as Skye and Princess greeted each other. "I'm so glad you and Princess are fine."

"We are and thanks so much to the MacNeills who have welcomed me into their home for the time being."

"I'm really glad for that. They've been great"—Alyth grasped Evander's hand and smiled at him—"especially, Evander."

"I see." Rebecca smiled at her. "So Skye's shenanigans haven't all been in vain."

"You're right," Alyth said as they headed for the great hall to have breakfast while one of the men escorted Princess and Skye to the kennel where they could run in the yard, just the two of them.

Then after they had breakfast, Alyth said she'd see Rebecca later, and Evander took her back to her house and kissed her. "I'll see you for lunch," he said, sure whatever happened at work, he was certain he could get someone to cover for him.

"I can't wait," she said, and kissed him before he left, their lips lingering a bit before they parted.

She waved goodbye and he got into his car and waved to her. She went back inside and shut the door.

He was feeling on top of the world until he saw a red car drive off from near the bakery. *The* red car? It was the same make and model. He hurried to jump into his car and tore off after the car. The driver might not have anything to do with trying to steal Skye, but Evander had to know one way or another.

But whoever the driver was had just vanished, taken a turn and disappeared before Evander could reach him. Damn it. Evander kept searching the whole area, but he couldn't find the car. Evander was sure the driver had tried to evade him, not just been at the bakery, left, and was on his way to somewhere without a care in the world.

Evander got on his phone and called Alyth.

"Evander, what's up?"

"I saw that red car again. I've been searching for it, but it got away from me. The way he or she took off, I feel it raises more questions about the person's culpability."

"Oh, I hadn't seen it for a while, so I thought maybe it wasn't anything. Did you get the license plate number?"

"No. The driver tore off so fast, I missed it."

"Okay. I'll keep an eye out for it if it returns and let you know," she said.

"Yeah, and I'll return if you see it. I'm headed back to the castle, and I'll let Ian know about it. He'll have someone out there keeping an eye on things. They let up their guard because Skye is staying at the castle now. I'll see you at lunch then." Evander called Ian right after that. "Hey, I spotted the red car again, but I lost it."

"I'll send some men to search for it again. We thought while Skye stayed at the castle or at your cottage, if someone was trying to grab her, they would realize she was no longer at Alyth's house and give up on it."

"Right, which means the red car might not have anything to do with a possible potential dog napping." Then Evander arrived at the castle and checked in with the dogs at the kennel, first with Shadow and her pups.

∾

NO ONE FOUND any sign of the red car while Evander and Alyth had kept Skye at the castle to protect her during the day. They washed her that night outside in the yard, each taking a side to soap up, but Alyth hadn't warned him that Skye liked to grab the hose. Before they could rinse her off, she grabbed it and ran across the yard. They laughed. While Evander and Alyth were trying to get the hose, Skye sprayed both of them. They were soaking wet as they tried to take the hose from her, grabbing her slippery, soapy body was futile, while she ran all over the yard, spraying water everywhere. Evander and Alyth were laughing so hard, she paused to hold her stomach and his hurt too.

"You planned that," Evander said, as he tried to take back control of the hose before Skye's teeth made holes in it.

"Not me. It must be your influence. She has never done that with me." Alyth was smiling too wickedly to be telling the truth, and he guessed differently.

"Oh, really."

She laughed. "Okay, maybe once or twice, but never to really play tug-of-war, or to get me, well, us, this wet and then make us chase her for it. I think she just wanted us to pay more attention to her."

"She has got it."

They were laughing so hard that Skye knew she was amusing them, and they weren't mad at her. She finally wore down and so did they and she dropped the hose, then took a drink of the water from the nozzle.

Skye was all soaped up still, and Evander took hold of the hose, glad it was really a sturdy construction, and began rinsing Skye off. "You know if I had just purchased this hose and wanted to review its good points, I would say it could withstand a Scottish deerhound's strong grip and didn't even leave toothy puncture marks."

Alyth laughed. "Then someone would say ask why we use it to play tug-of-war with the dog."

"Yeah. I'm sure we're not the only ones that have done that."

"I haven't bathed her in a while. Seeing us shower when she doesn't get to take part in it is sure to be the reason that she was playing with us."

He smiled and came over to the other side to rinse Skye off. They had a couple of large towels sitting on the chair on the patio and once Evander was done rinsing Skye off, he turned off the hose and wound it back up on its holder. Then Alyth and Evander began drying Skye and she loved all the attention she was getting.

"She is in heaven," Alyth said.

"She sure is with her favorite two people making her feel great. We'll have to schedule a bath for her before the puppies are due."

"Absolutely."

He'd never had so much fun washing a dog ever. Alyth, well, and Skye, had been perfectly entertaining.

They finally took Skye inside and Alyth started a load of wash while he dried Skye with a dryer. Once she was brushed and smelling like peaches and cream, they washed up, threw on some dry clothes, and made up a quick dinner of pizza.

"We're watching that Queen Ann historical series, right?" Alyth asked cutting up the pizza into slices.

"We sure are."

After dinner, feeding Skye and taking her out, Evander making sure she didn't roll in the grass to get rid of her sweet-smelling shampoo scent, they returned to the house and settled down to watch their show. They snuggled together as Skye laid down at their feet even though she had a giant-size bed a few feet away. It wasn't close enough to her people.

EVERY NIGHT, Evander and Alyth had dinner, watched their show, went to bed, made love, and the next morning Evander would take Skye back to the castle during the day while Alyth worked in her shop. Sometimes they all stayed at Evander's house at night. They planned to continue doing what they had been doing until the pups were born and went to their new homes. At least Skye was no longer in heat and could be around all the dogs, even Dillon, the stud.

Three weeks later, Skye's belly was larger, her teats enlarged and were darker. She was more tired now, eating more, vomiting sometimes with morning sickness, and she was trying to make a nest in Alyth's closet when she was at her house or in Evander's closet when she was at the cottage! But she was also constantly seeking affection as if Alyth and Evander could relieve her of the discomfort she was feeling.

Even if Alyth hadn't bred Skye to Magnus, she still could be having Dillon's puppies, which made her feel better about forcing this on Skye with Magnus breeding with her. Not that Skye hadn't wanted Magnus's attentions! And then Dillon's!

Evander had brought a whelping box for Skye and her puppies to Alyth's house in case she had the puppies there on one of the nights they were staying there. He put it in the guest bedroom and had it all set up with newspaper and old towels, perfect for Skye to have her puppies in a safe and out of the way place. But Skye kept moving the old towels to Alyth's closet. They were also prepared to have the puppies at the kennel, if she suddenly had them there while he was working with the other dogs. And he had a whelping box at his place. They had all their bets covered, he hoped. Though the last two nights, Skye had wanted to be at Alyth's home and had been too unsettled to stay with them at his cottage. Which meant late last night, they'd actually had to pack her up and all three of them had returned to Alyth's home. He sensed Skye was going to have her puppies soon.

The next day, Alyth worked as usual, but she and Nita were taking turns watching Skye, worried she'd have her pups while they were busy at the store. In fact, everyone had been dropping by to check on her from Lana to Julia, Ian, and even Heather's brothers. Evander was busy with the Irish wolfhounds, but he would stay with Alyth and Skye for dinner and through the night tonight and until the pups came.

After the shop was closed for the night, Alyth returned home and thanked Lana for watching Skye that last hour before closing before Evander arrived.

"I believe you're going to have pups real soon," Lana said, giving her a hug.

"I think so too." Alyth was both anxious and excited about it. Mostly because she hoped all the pups were in good health and that Skye would be fine and be a good mother. "Thanks so much, Lana." She gave her a hug in return and then Lana left.

Alyth wondered where Skye had disappeared in the house when she usually was nearby all the time. When she went to check on her, she found her in the master bedroom closet. Skye wagged her tail at her. "All right. I'll get some more towels for your nursery because you're going to have the puppies in the whelping box." She put some more rags in the box, then there was a knock on her door, and she hoped it was Evander. They had been having a blast with watching their favorite TV series, having dinner that she cooked, or that he ordered delivered, or he took her out, and then running as wolves through the woods or along the beach on the MacNeills' property every night, always having someone look after Skye while they were gone.

Alyth opened the door, Skye at her side, wagging her whole body to see her best friend again. This time, Evander was carrying a vase of roses and a box of fudge brownies. She smiled. "You are full of surprises. But you know you have a key to my place and—"

"My hands were totally full, and I couldn't get my keys out. Tonight is a celebration." He had even brought Skye a new ball —for after she had her puppies.

Alyth thought Evander was the cutest. She had made Evander salmon, his favorite dish—poached with lemon, white wine, and herbs–wanting this to be a special night. They were finishing up the end of a historical fiction series season finale and they had planned to celebrate. If he didn't ask her to mate him tonight, she was asking him. He was the bright spot in her life. He had taken her to all the MacNeill wolf pack functions, where everyone teased him that if he didn't mate her soon it would be too late as the bachelors were waiting in line to date her next—and she knew the bachelor males were not kidding— despite the lighthearted joking.

But she only wanted Evander. All her sexy dreams were of him, and all their hot, steamy nights told them they needed to go all the way, she felt. She wanted the hot consummated sex with him for real—a mating as wolves forevermore.

He loved Skye as if she were his own dog and that had endeared him to her right away. He always brought Skye special little treats and played with her every night after Alyth's store closed, until Skye had become too tired to play. He did the same thing when they were at his cottage and in the large yard surrounded by the ancient stone wall.

Tomorrow, the store wasn't open, and Alyth wanted Evander all the way tonight—in the worst way—so they would have all day tomorrow to be with each other alone as a mated couple.

"Hmm, salmon," Evander said, pulling Alyth into his arms to kiss her, but Skye wanted his attention too.

They were kissing, building up steam, tongues tangling,

Alyth's body pressed against Evander's when Skye nudged his back, making him chuckle.

"Oh, Skye," Alyth groaned. "Okay, take her out so she doesn't miss her nightly routine with you, and I'll start serving up the salmon. Talk about creatures of habit."

He chuckled. "Come on, Skye. Your momma and I are celebrating tonight."

Alyth smiled. *Really* celebrating if Evander was agreeable. She set out the white wine and the silverware and even though they didn't have to take Skye out on a leash any longer, Skye was feeling super needy, and she loved going out with Evander—her new boyfriend too.

After a few minutes, Evander came in with Skye and washed up and he and Alyth sat down to dinner.

"You make the best meals," he said.

"Thanks. And thanks for the flowers and chocolate." She loved how he was always bringing her flowers and gifts. He was so romantic. "And for the ball for Skye. She'll love it when she can play with it and her pups will probably too."

"Absolutely. So today is truly special. I wanted to tell you that you mean everything in the world to me, Alyth. A day doesn't go by that I'm not thinking about you—and what I want to happen between us."

She was going to wait for him to ask. She really was, but the anticipation was killing her. "A mating?"

He smiled. "Aye, beyond my wildest dreams I never thought I would find a she-wolf who I could fall in love with like I have with you. You're the only one for me. You filled a void I didn't even realize I had. I want to retire to bed and wake up to see your bright, cheerful face every day. I want you for my mate, now and forever."

"Oh, aye. I feel the same way about you. I was going to ask you if you didn't ask me tonight."

He laughed. "Good. I'm glad you don't want to wait either. Neither of us have parents any longer, though my twin sister, Lana, wants you to be part of our family too. I want to be your mate, to love you, and have our own wolf pups someday. Skye is part of our family already, and to tell you the truth, if you turned me down—well, I would do everything in my power to change your mind—but if that didn't work either, I would have to have visitation rights with Skye."

Alyth laughed, left her chair, and hugged him while he was trying to get out of his chair. "Aye, I will be your mate and you will have all the visitation rights you want. I love you, you big old wolf. I couldn't be more thrilled. And I'm so glad to have a sister in Lana."

He stood, wrapped his arms around her and then they were kissing again, and of course Skye got in on the act, nudging them with her muzzle, her tail whipping about it, knowing whatever was going on was important and she should be included. They laughed and both gave her hugs.

"Let's have our dinner so the salmon doesn't get cold, and we can watch the finale of our show a little later," Alyth said.

"I knew that was another reason I love you. When you have your mind made up to do something, it gets done," he said.

"Absolutely. The same with you." She didn't want to rush through dinner, feeling more relaxed now that she knew they were going to mate, and it would be done. She could barely wait, but she wanted him to enjoy his special dinner too.

They returned to their seats and toasted each other with their glasses of wine. "To many happy years," she said.

"Forever."

He already had moved a few clothes to her house, and she had some at his cottage for after their wolf runs and so she could play with Shadow's growing pups. He had been staying overnight at her house as much as he could, showing he didn't want to be without her. After last night and Skye's unease, they couldn't stay at his cottage right now because Skye was too anxious to go anywhere else but her own home and yard, even though it would be a while before she had her pups.

"About the living arrangements—" Alyth cut into her salmon.

"I'll move to your place. It's not far for me to travel back to the castle to take care of the dogs during the day while you're at the shop. In fact, I'll drop by to have lunches with you whenever I can. We can go out, or we can eat with the pack."

Evander didn't cook, just made sandwiches when he felt like it. But with a pack that had a cook who made their meals, he hadn't had any need to learn. She didn't mind. She loved to cook, and he loved her cooking. But she figured she'd get him an outdoor grill for Christmas, and he could learn to grill meals when the weather was nice. He'd dropped by the store a few times in the past few weeks at lunchtime also, and she figured it was because he couldn't stay away from her as much as she felt the same way about him. He was always buying Nita a lunch too, when he took Alyth out and Nita had teased him that if Alyth didn't work out for him, she was ready and available.

At the time, Alyth suspected she'd already stolen Evander's heart like he'd stolen hers.

Despite meaning to take her time and enjoy the meal, she and Evander were eating faster than they ever had, all conversation tabled so they could get to the important and fun part. She had already heeled off her pumps and she was certain she had heard him push his shoes off under the table while they were finishing up their meal. That was getting to be a routine for them, and then they would head to bed for unconsummated sex. Except this time, they would go all the way.

He waited a moment to watch her as she finished the last bite of her salmon and smiled.

"Everything was delicious," he said.

"Thanks. I know how much you love salmon."

As soon as she finished her food, he quickly moved from his seat as if he couldn't wait a second longer. She rose from hers and he lifted her up in his arms and she kissed his mouth, the passion between them igniting at once.

He carried her to the bedroom and set her on her feet and lightly brushed his lips against hers, his hands on her shoulders, caressing. Then he deepened the kiss, wild, and intoxicating. She responded with just as much enthusiasm. The heat of his body and his muscled hardness pressed against her, and her body tensed and tingled. She rubbed her breasts against his chest and felt his growing erection teasing her belly. She had no control over the way she felt whenever he wrapped his arms around her and held her close, kissing her, touching her, making her mad with desire. Her whole body blazed with need. His mouth moved from hers and over her jaw and throat, heating her blood, his hands moving from her hips to take hold of her breasts. He massaged her breasts and she felt uplifted and cherished, while she ran her hands down his backside and squeezed his firm ass.

His mouth pressed gentle kisses over her breastbone, and she sighed with pleasure.

Desire coursed through her as their heartbeats grew in intensity. His eyes were smoky with need as he paused to cup her face and peer down at her as if she was the most precious thing in the world to him. She smiled wickedly up at him and reached up to pull his face down to hers again. She kissed him thoroughly, the wine and herbs flavoring his tongue, their breaths shortening as she moved her body against his erection, declaring she wanted him, like she had for weeks.

They heard scratching in the closet and Evander and Alyth

chuckled, knowing their dog, because Skye was as much his as she was Alyth's now, was declaring the closet her nesting site.

Then Evander swept his hands down Alyth's body in a sexy way, reached for her blouse, and started to unbutton it. He began kissing her mouth again, his fingers struggling with the buttons. She was about ready to help him when he finished and pulled the blouse out of her tartan skirt's waistband, slipped it off her shoulders, and tossed it to a chair. The chair had become their nightly clothes tree.

"Hmm, hot red lace for a hot-blooded she-wolf." He ran his hands over her lacy bra and gently squeezed her breasts. He seemed to appreciate her selection of a bra. She'd purposefully worn a red one for today, wanting to look sexier for her wolf, instead of wearing a plain white one that she often wore. And he seemed to love the way it looked on her. His tongue teased her nipples through the lace bra, and then he kissed them, her nipples needy for his touch. The best part about the bra was it fastened in front, and he soon discovered that and opened it, then removed the bra so he could kiss and lick her nipples further, making her heart race and her skin heat.

She moved her hands down his well-sculpted pecs and slipped her hands underneath his shirt, sliding her fingers up his bare chest, her thumbs teasing his nipples. He quickly slipped his hands beneath her buttocks and pulled her hard against his burgeoning erection—that she had caused.

"Hmm." She licked his chin, then pulled off his shirt so she could lick his nipples and she did and nibbled on them.

He groaned and tightened his hands on her hips. "I love you, lass," he said, his voice tense with need. "I want your whole heart, to be the only man in your life."

"I know."

He chuckled.

"I love you too. And I want your whole heart back and to be

the only woman in your life." Then she started to work on his belt.

He did the same with hers and had it undone first, letting her skirt drop to the floor. Then she pulled his pants off, and he quickly threw his pants and her skirt on the chair. She appreciated that he knew how important her clothes were because she modeled them in the store, and it always helped sales.

She was about to push him on the bed—it was a contest to see who went down first and then tackled socks. But as soon as she raised her hands to push him onto the bed, he maneuvered quickly to sweep her up in his arms and deposit her on the bed. Then he was pulling off one of her socks, and then the other. He didn't wait for her to get his, but quickly yanked them off himself.

Then he was on top of her, kissing her, pressing his rigid erection against her mound, telling her without words that he was past ready to mate with her. She was past ready too, loving the feel of him against her, experiencing the most beautiful connection with the wolf, loving him. They were writhing against each other, sharing their scent, claiming each other in a wolf way. Increasing the friction, she felt the heat rising, their pheromones pumping up. Telling each other that they were meant for each other and no one else.

From the first time she'd met him, she'd been impressed with the way he'd helped her with Skye, but there was so much more to him than that. And she wanted to keep every bit of him for herself!

They were kissing again, though he was sliding off her and yanking his boxer briefs off. Then he slid her red panties down her legs and began kissing her again, their mouths clinging, tongues teasing. He swept his hand down her belly and began to stroke her nub. Every stroke brought her higher as she swept her hands down his back, but her concentration was on his glorious touch. He knew just how to prime her in a way that had maximum effect. She moaned with the way his strokes were making her wet with desire, readying her for his penetration. The way he was sending her out of the galaxy, climbing to that point of no return.

Maybe it was her intake of breath, barely breathing, her heart racing, but somehow, he knew just when she was going to climax, and he covered her mouth with his. He kissed her soundly as the orgasm hit her full force so she wouldn't cry out and upset Skye like she'd done before. Then he moved Alyth's legs apart and she was ready to be mated with the wolf of her dreams.

He didn't need to ask if she was ready for this. He could smell her need and desire, see the look of expectation in her expression, knew she wouldn't have it any other way.

As soon as he was on top of her, easing in, inch by delectable inch, and pushing all the rest of the way, she relaxed and began moving with him. She stroked his waist and arched to increase the penetration, experiencing the oneness wolves felt when they finally mated. She couldn't be happier.

He was kissing her again, his mouth warm and masculine and possessive and she felt desirable and well-loved. She licked the seam of his mouth, gaining entrance, and then shared long, gliding licks with hungry passion. She was so glad they hadn't waited any longer to do this. Buried to the hilt, Evander began to thrust in earnest, and she gave into the pure pleasure of the mating.

10

Evander loved Alyth and was ready to howl at the moon, he was so lucky to have found her to mate. Beautiful, funny, smart, fun to be with, and sexy to the max. His heart was beating as hard as hers as he thrust into her in their mating coupling, their pheromones doing an exotic dance. She was arching against him, and he was afraid he was going to spill his seed too soon. She was divine, every inch of her —her soft, sweet skin, her well-shaped muscles, her silky, long, dark hair spread out against the pillow, blue eyes the color of the sky now smoky with desire, her tongue slipping out to lick her lips. He kissed her again, gently, but the passion between them took over, and he thrust between her legs deeply again. Then he slowed his thrusts, wanting to hold off on the inevitable, reminding himself he could make love to her all night long for the rest of their lives. But he still wanted to pleasure her again, to make her come.

He felt her breathing hitch and he thought she was ready to come again. He couldn't hold off any longer. Not with the way she smelled, and tasted, and felt, her soft breath barely audible. He thrust until the end, exploding deep inside her, and he felt her tense. He continued to thrust until she was ready to cry out. He caught her cry with his mouth and kissed her. Never would he have thought he would have to quiet his lover's cry of pleasure to keep their dog from worrying that Alyth was okay.

"God, how I love you, Alyth."

"You are mine, all mine, Evander. I love you."

Forget about the finale of their TV series. They could watch it anytime. They were spending the rest of the night in each other's arms, loving each other.

Then Skye pawed at the bed, telling them she needed to relieve herself outside. So much for staying in bed together for the rest of the night and not leaving it for anything!

Evander was still taking her out because they worried about someone stealing her, and he wanted to be there if they had any trouble.

He threw on his boxer briefs, then he took an eager Skye outside. She was taking her time looking for the right spot to relieve herself as usual, circling, sniffing at the ground, moving on, while Evander was trying to be patient with her when he wanted to be in bed with Alyth. Suddenly, he heard something at the fence. He watched the fence, listening, until he heard the sound again. But Skye still hadn't done her business.

"Hurry up, Skye. Do your thing."

She just looked at him and wagged her tail.

He sighed. No more distracting the dog. He glanced again at the fence. No sounds over that way now, though he planned to check it out. He just wished Skye hurried up with her business. Then, thank the heavens, Skye relieved herself and Evander took her inside the house and closed the back door. But he went straight through the house and out the front door where he found someone trying to peer through the slats of the fence.

Evander rushed the middle-aged man and tackled him to the ground. "Who are you and what are you doing here?" He was so mad, figuring this was the potential dog thief they hadn't been able to catch before now.

"You have my dog! Get off me! She was stolen from me. That's my dog, Misty!" The man scowled at Evander, his blue eyes hard with condemnation.

"What?" Here Evander truly believed he'd caught the dog thief, unless this was an attempt at making up a halfway plausible story for the guy spying on Skye.

"My dog, Misty. She has a double champion parentage; both her mom and dad are champs."

"Double champion parentage?" That was kind of uncommon, and for the same breed of dog as Skye was? Immediately Evander thought of Skye's parents. "Who's the breeder and what is the dam's name?"

"Rebecca Johnson, the owner of the dam and Princess was Misty's mother. Blue Boy is the father." The man brushed a tangle of unruly brown hair out of his eyes.

"Ah, hell. Well, Skye, that's Alyth's dog, is from the same breeder and dam and sire. Maybe your dog and hers were even from the same litter." If the guy wasn't lying to him about all this.

"Two and a half years old?"

"Aye," Evander said. "I'm Evander Cameron and my fiancée, Alyth MacBain, owns Skye."

"I'm Samuel Lemming and I hope this is all a horrible mistake, though I truly believed I'd found Misty."

"It is, but I hope we can help you find your dog." Evander pulled his phone out of his pocket and called Alyth. "I caught a man peeking through your fence and he's the one we figured was trying to grab Skye. He thought Skye was his dog that was stolen from him."

"Misty," Samuel said, looking exasperated. "That's *my* dog's name."

"His dog's name is Misty, and she might be from the same litter as Skye. He had the same breeder and Princess was his dog's mother."

"Och, I'm coming out. I'll just put something on."

Evander really hoped they could get this matter cleared up and maybe they would no longer have to worry about someone stealing Skye. Though if this man lived somewhere nearby and his deerhound had been stolen, then that wasn't good either. And he did want to help Samuel get his dog back too.

A few minutes later, Alyth came out of the house, brushing her hair out of her face and frowning at the man. "If your dog was born in March, two and a half years ago, then she *was* from Skye's litter and Princess was her mother and Blue Boy was the daddy."

"That sounds right. Can I see your dog up close?" Samuel asked.

"I'll get her," Alyth went back inside the house and brought Skye out on her leash. "When was your dog stolen?" She sounded sympathetic toward the man, when Evander wasn't feeling quite that way yet. Not after all that he'd put them through.

"A month ago."

"About the same time that we assumed someone was trying to steal Skye," Alyth said. "Well, actually you, it seems."

"I thought you had stolen or... well, uh, had purchased my stolen dog. Misty looks just like Skye."

"Is Misty microchipped?" Evander asked.

"Aye. I was going to take this dog to the vet and have them scan her microchip to verify if she was Misty."

"Well, she isn't. And you could have just asked," Alyth said, annoyed with him at that point.

"If you had paid a good price for her, you could have said you had always owned her and you didn't want to give her up,"

Samuel countered. "Not to mention it's easy to fall in love with them and you wouldn't want to hand her over for that reason either."

"Well, I have owned her since she was six weeks old. At least that's when I bought her. I took her home when she was eight weeks old. I would have been willing to go with you to see a vet and have Skye's microchip scanned to prove she was mine. *Hold on.* I don't have to prove anything to you, but I understand you need to know this for your own peace of mind. I have the papers and pictures of her and the pictures of her littermates." Alyth went back into the house.

"I'm sorry for all this," Samuel said, his eyes filled with tears. A couple slid down his cheek and he quickly brushed them away as if he was afraid Evander would notice them.

"I'm sorry someone stole your dog, but Alyth's right. You could have talked to us, and we would have sorted this out without all the cloak and dagger business," Evander said, holding onto Skye's leash while she sat down obediently next to him. He didn't like that the man had taken such measures and scared Alyth, but he understood how he felt about losing his dog.

"She's going to have pups," Samuel said, looking at Skye's expanded belly.

"Aye, in another four weeks."

Then Alyth finally came outside with Skye's birth certificate and other papers, shot records, and pictures of Skye at various ages. She pointed to a photo of Princess's litter of pups when they were six weeks old. "Look at this photo of the pups. These two are practically identical."

"That's Misty," the man said, pointing to the pup next to Skye. He looked at Skye. "Their coloration is a little different. Misty has a little whiter face. And Skye is devoted to you. I can tell she doesn't recognize me."

"Exactly. If she was Misty, she would have practically wagged her tail off and greeted you like crazy," Alyth said.

Samuel wiped away several more tears. "Aye, you're right. I'm sorry. I've been looking for Misty for the last month. I was sure Skye was her. I apologize if I scared you."

"You did. I was afraid you had intended to steal her. Do you live around here?" Alyth asked.

"About fifteen miles away."

This was worrisome because that wasn't all that far from Alyth's place. "How did you learn about Skye?" Evander asked.

"I saw Alyth and Skye at the Coach House where she was eating, and they were serving water and treats to her dog shortly after Misty was stolen, like two days later. I swore it was Misty. But I couldn't confront her there. I followed her home and from then on, I was trying to catch a better look at her."

"You planned to steal her," Evander said, wanting Samuel to say what he truly meant.

"Only to verify she was my dog. If she hadn't been, I would have returned her."

Alyth's phone suddenly rang, and she pulled it out of her pocket. Looking surprised, she said to Evander, "It's Cal." She answered the phone then. "Hello, Cal." She put it on speakerphone.

"We're halfway to the end now before Skye has her puppies. How is she doing?"

Evander was surprised Cal would call to check on her. Maybe because he now sort of had a vested interest in her if he took one of the puppies for the stud fee. Or maybe even that he wondered if Alyth and Evander were still dating.

"She's doing great. She has had a little morning sickness, and she's more tired now, but otherwise, she's fine. Thanks for calling to check on her." She glanced at Samuel. "I have a question for you though. Has Magnus or any of your other stud dogs serviced any other dams from Princess and Blue Boy's litter?"

"Yeah, two others. It's funny you should ask that. One looked so much like Skye, I thought it was her when I brought Magnus to breed with her at your place. I was wondering what was going on at first."

"Really. Could you tell me who the owner is?" Alyth asked.

"Benji Ryder. He lives about twenty-five miles from you. His dam came in heat at the same time as Skye, and she had the same papers showing her birth and parentage, so I knew they were from the same litter."

"When he stole Misty, did he take her papers too?" Evander asked Samuel.

"What?" Cal asked.

"Sorry, it appears Misty was stolen from her rightful owner," Alyth explained to Cal.

"Yeah. I had Misty's papers sitting out on the dining room table because I was going to contact Cal Sutherland about breeding her," Samuel said. "I guess this guy decided to steal my dog and beat me to it."

"Do you know him? I mean, how did he learn about your dog and that she was a good choice to breed?" Alyth asked.

"I've posted about her on social media. Maybe that's how," Samuel said, sounding angry about it. "I mean, she's so cute, it's hard not to post about her."

"Well, hell," Cal said. "So this Benji Ryder doesn't own Misty?"

"No. He stole her," Samuel said.

"Do you have documentation about her like Alyth has of Skye other than the birth papers?" Evander asked.

"Yeah, the photos and such, but not the rest of the documents because he stole them. But she's also wearing a microchip."

Evander pulled out his phone. "I'm calling the police." Then he said, "Hi, I'm Evander Cameron and we believe we've discovered the location of a friend's stolen Scottish deerhound. The legitimate owner is Samuel Lemming. We need to have her checked out at the vet so they can read the microchip implanted in her." Evander gave the officer the name of the person who had Misty and the address.

"And you know all this, how?" the officer asked.

Evander explained about the breeder who had bred his dog to Misty. He told the officer that Skye was from the same litter, and how Samuel thought she might be his dog, which was how they learned about his dog being stolen. But Evander left out the part about Samuel trying to steal Skye to learn if she was Misty. "If it's all right with you, we would like to meet you there."

"Aye, sure."

"I'll call my vet to see if she'll bring her scanner to read the microchip," Samuel said.

Evander relayed the information to the officer.

"Okay. I'll meet you there then," the officer said.

Evander ended the call with the officer.

"I would love to go with you, but someone has to stay and watch over Skye," Alyth said.

"Are you all right with me going?" Evander didn't want Alyth to believe he was abandoning her, but he wanted to see this resolved. Because Samuel had been so sure Skye was his dog, he didn't want any more trouble with him.

"Aye. I'll be glad to learn that Samuel gets his Misty back," Alyth said.

Full of pups, most likely, Evander was thinking.

Cal, still on the line with Alyth, said, "Let me know what happens with all this."

"We will," Evander said.

Then Alyth ended the call with Cal and kissed Evander. She

took hold of Skye's leash and said, "I'll see you soon. Good luck, Samuel."

"Yeah, uh, I'm so sorry for trying to take Skye though my intentions were good," Samuel said.

"I understand how you felt, and I realize you might have been afraid to confront me in the event I was bad news," Alyth said.

"Yeah. I figured you were either part of the gang who stole her or had bought her from the thief, unbeknownst to you. Dog napping is big business. But I could have done what Evander did and called the police and straightened this out right away," Samuel said, sounding sincerely apologetic.

"Well, I hope you learn that Benji has Misty and that he gets charged and time in jail for stealing your dog," Alyth said.

"Me too. Thanks." Then Samuel said he would follow Evander over to Benji's house, driving that red car they had seen before while Alyth returned to the house with Skye.

Evander said, "I'll get dressed and be right out." He couldn't believe this turn of events and he sure hoped all this would be resolved. Though after this had happened, they would continue to ensure Skye stayed safe and no one tried to grab her.

When they finally arrived at the gray stone house where Benji lived, they had to wait for the police officer to arrive. They stopped across the street at a park that surrounded a pond where ducks and geese mingled. Lamp lights cast reflections off the still water.

Then they got out of their cars and watched for the officer to show up.

"I mean it when I say that I'm sorry for scaring Alyth."

"She knows," Evander said. "And she truly understands. I think she's just relieved more than anything that you aren't a dog thief intent on stealing Skye."

Then the officer arrived, and Evander and Samuel waved to

him. Another car drove up and parked near Samuel's car. Then a woman got out.

"That's my vet." Samuel quickly shook her hand. "Thanks so much for coming, Dr. Brandt."

"Sure thing. Anything to help out."

Then they all went over to speak to the police officer, everyone introducing themselves before the officer talked to Benji. They heard a dog bark inside and then a chorus of wild barking, from little dog woofs to large dog barks and everything in between.

How many dogs were living there?

Then a man came to the door, nice-looking, in-shape, dark haired, clean shaven, dressed in jeans, boots, and a short-sleeved shirt. He sure didn't look like what Evander had expected a dog thief to look like—frumpy, unshaven, baggy clothes, dumpy. He looked like he had the means to own a dog like Misty and be able to pay Cal's stud fee. And he probably would if he was stealing a lot of dogs and getting paid for them.

"Are you Benji Ryder?" the officer asked.

"What's this all about?" Benji asked, sounding shocked, not like he felt guilty.

But Evander smelled Benji's deception and concern right away. Evander texted Princess's owner, Rebecca, and told her that they had probably located Misty, one of Princess's pups from Skye's litter sold to Samuel Lemming that had been stolen.

Rebecca texted back: *Oh, no. Do you need me to identify Samuel as the owner?*

Evander texted: *Aye, that would be great.*

He sent Rebecca the address.

"Do you have a Sottish deerhound on the premises," the officer asked Benji.

"Yeah. What's this all about?" Benji asked again.

"This gentleman," the officer said, motioning to Samuel,

"believes that the dog you have is his dog, so we need to see the dog and have his vet scan the dog's microchip."

"I can't believe this. What proof do you have?" Benji asked, as if they had no right scanning the chip.

"A breeder has verified he has bred his stud dog to Misty, who has the same parents as Mr. Lemming's dog."

"Does he have proof?" Benji asked again.

"The owner of the dam who sold the dog to Samuel, Rebecca Johnson," Evander said. "She's living at the MacNeill castle right now. She can identify Samuel as Misty's owner. And she's on her way to see you now."

"Okay, listen, I bought this dog from a woman and—" Benji started to say, his expression one of anxiousness and it appeared he was trying to change his story right away.

"Do you have proof that you bought the dog? What was the woman's name?" Before Benji could answer the officer, the officer said, "Either bring her out so the vet can identify her or let the vet and me into the house to scan Misty's microchip."

Benji started into the house and the officer put his foot inside the doorway to stop the guy from shutting the door.

Evander suspected the officer didn't trust Benji, which was smart since the guy was probably up to his eyeballs in stolen dogs.

Once the vet verified that Misty was Samuel's dog, the officer brought her out on a leash and Misty was so excited to see Samuel, they all knew she was Samuel's dog. They also saw the way he was so thrilled to have her back.

The officer again asked if Benji had a Bill of Sale for the purchase of Misty.

"Yeah, but I must have misplaced it," Benji said.

"What about the birth papers? Mr. Sutherland, the stud dog owner, said you showed them to him," the officer said.

"I've got those."

Evander suspected that Benji thought the officer might reconsider the whole matter if he showed him the papers. The officer went into the house with Benji and then returned with the paperwork. The officer handed it to Samuel. Benji brows rose, and his jaw dropped at the same time.

The officer asked Benji, "Can you show me a bank statement that shows you purchased Misty from Mr. Lemming?"

"Like I said, I'm kind of disorganized. I have the paperwork in the house somewhere."

The officer raised a brow. "You have nothing online that you can show me? A cashed check from your bank? A bank account that shows a check was written and to whom? I'll tell you what —" He stopped speaking when another car pulled up.

Rebecca got out of her car, her eyes widening when she saw Benji and said, "I'm—"

"Rebecca Johnson and the owner of my dog's dam," Benji said, stealing everyone's thunder.

"Uhm, this gentleman, Samuel Lemming, purchased Misty from me. Unless Samuel sold her to—" Rebeca said.

"I never sold her. She was stolen from my yard," Samuel said.

"Okay, then Samuel owns the dog," Rebecca said, "and this man needs to be arrested for stealing Samuel's dog." She spoke as an authority on the matter. But then she dropped the real bombshell. "And he"—she motioned to Benji—"needs to be arrested for attempting to steal *my* dog." She told the officer the date and location where Benji had attempted to take Princess, and how she had thwarted him. "I'm sure if you investigate it further, though he was wearing a mask, you can see where I hit him on the side of the head with a walking stick when he broke into my house and tried to steal Princess."

Evander knew she had smelled his scent and that's what had to have really clued her in.

The officer said, "Benji Ryder, you're under arrest as a

suspect in the theft of two dogs." But then as an afterthought he asked, "What about the other dogs on the premises?"

They sure didn't want to leave the other dogs Benji had in the house and yard unattended. But what if they were not even his? What if they all had been stolen? Evander figured that was a good bet.

"I don't know what you mean, officer." Benji had the I-don't-know-anything down pat.

The officer put him in his patrol car, then went inside to check it out. He ended up calling the Scottish Society for the Prevention of Cruelty to Animals to come and pick up the large group of dogs—all pure bred, from Scottish terriers to two black male Labrador retrievers—if they were unable to locate the owners. He also called in more police officers to search Benji's premises to locate anything that would prove Benji had stolen the dogs.

After another officer arrived and they gave their story to him, they were all free to go.

"What are you going to do about Misty being pregnant?" Evander asked Samuel.

"I guess I'm going to be paying Cal Sutherland a stud fee, if Benji hadn't already paid for it, and taking care of a bunch of Scottish deerhound pups," Samuel said. "Though I would have anyway, since I had planned to breed her. I'll call Cal after I return Misty home. But from now on, I'll keep a stricter eye on Misty to ensure she's not stolen again. And thanks for all your help with this. Tell Alyth I apologize to her again for scaring her."

"I will. I'm glad you resolved your dog theft case also," Evander said to Rebecca.

"Yeah, me too. I never expected that to happen in a million years. Live and learn."

The vet hung around to check out all the dogs Benji had in

his house to make sure they were healthy, scanned their microchips, and found the homeowners' names and their addresses. She probably had never expected to be identifying a bunch of stolen dogs and she seemed concerned, relieved, and happy to have helped at the same time. The same with the officer.

Which made Evander wonder just how many dogs this guy had stolen over the years and gotten away with it. Or if he had ever been caught before and only got a slap on the wrist and was right back in business.

The great news was the officers were calling the owners of all the microchipped dogs to see if they still owned the dogs and Evander figured they would be ecstatic to get their beloved pets back. If it hadn't been for Evander wanting to return to Alyth and Skye, he would love to see the owners come for their pets and the happy reunions, if the officers and SPCA could reach them.

Then everyone said their goodbyes and they headed back to their places. Evander called Alyth on the way home. "Hey, honey, I'll be home in about a half hour."

"What happened?"

"Samuel was reunited with Misty, and both were over-whelmed to see each other. Even without learning Misty was truly Samuel's dog, just seeing them reunited proved it. Samuel will call Cal and tell him he's paying for the stud fee if Benji hasn't already. That's not the only good news though. Benji was also responsible for stealing fifteen other dogs that he had in the house, and he was the one who had tried to steal Princess."

"Oh, no. I can't believe it. What a bastard. I'm so glad they caught him. I hope the dogs are all okay."

"Samuel's vet was there identifying all the dogs and their owners and checking them out so they should be returned soon, and a lot of stolen dog cases will be cleared up, not to mention a lot of ecstatic pet owners when they get their fur babies home."

"That's truly wonderful. And it's all because Samuel had tried to steal Skye. Which in retrospect turned out to be a good thing. Well, that you caught him at it, at least. You didn't tell the police officer that, did you?" Alyth asked, sounding concerned for Samuel.

"No, and he apologized again."

"I wish I had seen their reunion."

"I know. It was gratifying. He was in tears."

"What about you?"

Evander laughed. "I might have been a little misty eyed myself. I knew just how he was feeling."

When he finally arrived home, he wanted to sweep Alyth up and take her to bed, but after Skye greeted him, she had to go outside to relieve herself again. That was the problem with a pregnant dog who was halfway through her pregnancy.

Alyth came out with them and just smiled as he waited for Skye to find just the right spot. He smiled at her, adoring her. She smiled back, looking ready to retire to bed and have her way with him. He certainly was ready to make love to his mate.

11

Thirty days later, Evander and Alyth were enjoying mated bliss at their home behind the shop waiting for Skye to have her first pup any time now. Twenty-four hours earlier, her rectal temperature had dropped from 101 degrees, normal for a dog, to 99. Nita said she was fine with managing the shop on her own, though Lana arrived at the shop to help her out, which Nita and Alyth were glad for.

Evander was Alyth's true hero, and Skye's, as he had everything set up to take care of the pups before they made their entrance into the world. Alyth would never have been able to manage, she didn't think, without someone's help who actually knew how to do this.

One adjustment they'd had to make? The whelping box ended up in their closet, not the guest bedroom's even, but theirs. That was Skye's den, and Alyth and Evander were her pack mates, protecting her and her pups—when they came—from the rest of the world outside her den.

Alyth and Evander had even moved some of their clothes and shoes into the guest room closet, just so they wouldn't have to disturb her when they were getting dressed in the mornings.

Evander said once the puppies were a little older, they could move her into the other room, like they'd planned.

For now, Skye was pacing, panting, refusing to eat. She settled into her box, and they thought the first puppy was coming, but then she began pacing again.

They talked to her, comforted her, then finally Skye settled back in the whelping box and pushed out the first puppy. The little female looked just like Shadow's pups, same size, same color. There was no way of telling if they were Magnus's or Dillon's. Evander took care of the first puppy and once he was done with the umbilical cord, Alyth cleaned her. She was so glad she could help with this and was grateful she knew what to do after assisting Evander with Shadow's puppies. Then she set Skye's first pup down to find Momma's milk and Alyth praised Skye and stroked her bony head. "You're doing so good. Just keep going."

But then Skye got up and Alyth rescued the puppy and put it in the laundry basket that Evander had brought over for the puppies. It was going to be a long day, a radiograph confirming she was carrying fourteen puppies. Nita already had claimed one, whether they were mixed breed or not. Alyth was giving it to her for free because of all the work she did for her.

By the time lunch rolled around, Julia arrived to bring Alyth and Evander lunch, and watch over Skye. "Cook made it. I'll take care of the momma and puppies."

Skye wagged her tail at Julia. She, Heather and her brothers, Lana, Nita, and Ian and his brothers, were all considered to be Skye's extended pack—as far as she was concerned. So any of them were a welcome sight.

Alyth and Evander thanked Julia, washed up, and began eating the ham and cheese sandwiches Cook had made for them. And he'd even sent a little cake for each of them too to celebrate Skye's puppies.

"That was sweet of Cook," Alyth said, not expecting the pack to help out so much as if one of their own wolves had just given birth. She realized that they would have plenty of assistance when the time came for that also as much as the pack members helped each other out. Everyone in the pack was thrilled Alyth and Evander had mated, all because of a couple of horny, runaway dogs.

As soon as they were done with lunch and dessert, they headed back to the closet that had become the whelping room. Everyone in the pack had thought it was funny that they hadn't been able to convince her to stay in the guest room.

"She has had another, a little female," Julia said, and Evander helped to finish up with the umbilical cord and Alyth cleaned up the pup. "That makes four. I'm out of here, but if you need anything else, just let me know."

"Thanks so much, Julia. I really appreciate it." Alyth had never expected her to come to help out, but Alyth had been selling her books, so Julia was totally grateful.

An hour later, Nita came to check on things. Two more pups. "Oh, they're so adorable. I can't choose."

"You don't have to pick one until they're older and you can see their real personality and more what they look like. We're not done yet either. Several more pups to go," Alyth said.

That evening, they thought Skye had the last of her pups, but she was still panting, pacing, and acting as though she was going to have more. That night, she had the last of the pups, fifteen in all, so the radiograph had been off by one.

It was nine that night by then, but Evander and Alyth took a shower together and then went to bed. One thing about having the puppies in the closet, they could hear them if there was any trouble while they were sleeping. Alyth had unlocked the dog door six weeks ago so Skye could go out to the backyard whenever she wanted to relieve herself.

But in the middle of the morning when Skye left the bedroom to go outside, they heard the puppies crying and whimpering for Mom. Alyth got out of bed to check on them and found two out of the box that Mom had carried with her on her teats, apparently. Alyth put them back with the other puppies. Everything was nice and warm in there and then they fell asleep before Skye anxiously returned to be with her pups.

"Well," Alyth said, climbing into bed with Evander and he pulled her into his arms to cuddle. "Next trip to check on the pups is yours."

He smiled. "I'll be happy to take care of them anytime. You just jumped out of bed too quickly before I had a chance to wake and take care of them this time."

They were also having to help feed them because the sheer number warranted it.

She loved that about Evander and snuggled closer to him. He was always there to share in any of the duties that needed to be done. And he was always ready to make love to her.

～

A WEEK LATER, they finally convinced Skye to sleep with her puppies in the guest room. Alyth and Evander sent in the DNA samples right after the pups were born to learn if they were Dillon's or Magnus's and the vet called with the results. Alyth put it on speakerphone.

"Well, depending on what you wanted to hear, it's good news or half good news," the vet said. "Eight of the pups are half-Irish wolfhound and half-Scottish deerhound, and seven of the pups are pure Scottish deerhound."

"What?" Alyth said, so shocked, she couldn't understand it.

"Well, if one dam breeds with a couple of dogs, they can end up having pups from both matings. So in this case, I take it Skye got away from you and met up with an Irish wolfhound?"

"Aye." She laughed. "It's all good. We love them all."

"We do," Evander said, looking a little smug that Dillon had more pups than Magnus.

"Thanks so much." Then they ended the call after she told the vet how the pups and mom were doing. Smiling, she hugged Evander. "Can you believe it?"

"Aye. Dillon's were faster swimmers."

She laughed.

"Are you disappointed?" Evander sounded a little worried and kissed her mouth.

She shook her head. "I'm just so surprised. I adore them. And I adore Skye and Dillon. And Cal can still take one of the puppies for payment or his stud fee. He won't be coming to see them until they're six weeks old. Two weeks later, they'll be ready to go home and then he can decide."

"Won't he be surprised to learn that a mix of pups are in the litter? And that Dillon had more pups out of the bargain?" Evander smiled as though it had been a competition.

"I'm just glad they're all healthy and hopefully we can find homes for all of them." She smiled and kissed him.

"We will."

SIX WEEKS LATER, Skye's pups were underfoot constantly. Most were around three feet in length and weighing thirteen pounds. Because there were fifteen of them, they were a handful. But Alyth and Evander adored each and every one of them. Even though they couldn't go home for a couple of more weeks, Nita had already picked out her Dillon and Skye puppy. She loved one that was darker than the rest with a white blaze down her forehead, but she was going to have her spayed when she was old enough. And Evander and Alyth had picked out Dillon's puppy that they wanted to keep also, a female that looked like a combination of Dillon and Skye that they called Chiffon. She was the sweetest little blue deerhound and brindle wolfhound combination.

They had just finished feeding all the pups and Skye and then had some breakfast when Alyth got a call. "It's Cal." She answered the call. "Hi, Cal, are you ready to choose a puppy?" She paused and smiled at Evander. "All right. I'll see you then."

When she finished the call, Evander asked, "When is Cal coming over? I'll be here so that he doesn't give you any grief."

"Ha! He might give you grief because Dillon had more puppies with Skye. He's coming here in an hour."

"I'll just hang around then."

"You don't have to if you have anything else you need to do."

"Yeah, I do."

"Okay. I'm glad." She didn't want him to feel like he had to if he was busy, but she was glad he would stay here with her. She probably should have told Cal that some of the pups weren't Magnus's, but she figured it didn't matter. If he didn't like the seven that were, they would just pay him the stud fee. When she had first bred Skye, she had never expected she would have such a hot wolf as her mate who would be there for her at all times. And being a daddy to all those pups? Oh, man, she was so lucky. He was always there, helping to feed the puppies and Skye seven to eight times a day. He also went in to work to handle the Irish wolfhounds but was always at home at lunchtime to help feed the dogs and take them out.

They took the pups and Skye out to relieve themselves and then the pups were biting and tackling each other. Evander rubbed Alyth's back while they enjoyed watching them play. "We haven't gone running as wolves for a while," he said.

"Yes, I agree. Maybe tonight?"

"Aye, sounds good to me."

"I'm going to the shop until Cal arrives if you can handle everything at the house in the meantime."

"Oh, you know I will." He kissed her soundly, and she hummed her pleasure. He always made her feel like a million pounds.

Then she headed to the shop and soon was helping Nita with the customers.

"How's my puppy doing?" Nita asked.

"She is holding her own. She takes down the biggest boys in the litter. You're going to have a fun one on your hands."

"And yours?" Nita asked, putting out some more teas and jars of honey.

"Oh, she's right in there with her. The two are a couple of characters. Cal will be coming over to take his pick of the litter, unless he decides he doesn't have enough to choose from, and he wants his stud fee."

"How do you feel about it?"

"I'm fine with either. We have sold all the mixed breed puppies. And made way more than enough to pay for the stud fee. And we'll have more when we sell the others. We had to wait until Cal takes his pick, if he does, before we offered the deerhounds for sale."

"I'm so happy for you," Nita said. "Mostly because Evander came with the deal."

Alyth smiled. "I know, right? He's a real match made in heaven." Alyth was busy with online orders when a busload of tourists arrived and she was helping Nita in the shop after that, but when she finally heard Cal's van drive up, she couldn't really leave the shop. She quickly texted Evander: *Cal's all yours to deal with.*

Evander texted back: *I've got this.*

She smiled. She knew he would have, then she was back to helping a second busload of tourists with their purchases.

WHEN CAL ARRIVED at the house, he appeared a little surprised that Evander was answering the door. Then Cal nodded, like he figured out why. "Two tour buses are parked at the shop."

"Aye. Alyth said I could handle it. We're mated, if you didn't know."

"No, I didn't. Congratulations. So where are the pups?" Cal was abrupt, business as usual.

"They're in here." They'd had to make a playroom for the pups, though they had run of the house also. Deerhounds really needed to be with their family. Even if they went outside for a while, they needed human companionship.

"Where are the rest of the pups? There are only seven here. Alyth can't sell any until I have the pick of the *entire* litter," Cal said, as if he assumed she was hiding the rest of them from him.

"Okay, so here's the thing. Skye mated with one of the MacNeills' Irish wolfhounds. So eight are Dillon's offspring, and seven are Magnus's."

His eyes wide, Cal folded his arms, appearing peeved, like he thought they might be trying to pull a fast one on him.

"You bred Magnus to Skye the night before she had her way with Dillon and then Magnus bred with her that night."

"Your champion? On purpose?"

"Of course not. So you have seven deerhounds to choose from. Now, Alyth and I are perfectly fine paying you the stud fee since you have fewer dogs to make your choice from. It's up to you."

"How in the hell did Skye get out and get with Dillon? Had

she visited the MacNeill's castle and...wait, does this have something to do with that bastard who stole Misty?"

"It does. He tried to steal Skye but only managed to get the gate open and then he got spooked." Evander didn't say that Samuel was the one who had done that. "Alyth let Skye into the yard before she realized the gate was open. So it wasn't Alyth's fault." Evander wasn't going to mention to Cal that Dillon had actually found Skye's home and wanted to love on her some more even after that.

"All right. Let me see the pups. And I want to see the others," Cal said, walking with Evander to one of the rooms.

"Don't you trust us?" Evander was amused.

"I'm just curious as to how similar they look to the full breed deerhounds."

Evander suspected Cal didn't trust them. And he believed that Cal would decide on having a stud fee. When Cal looked over the pups, they were so excited to see him, Evander swore that was the only time he'd seen Cal smile. He finally glanced back at Evander who was watching him with the pups, though he was crouched down petting a couple of them while they tried to chew on his fingers.

"It's impossible not to love them all. I'll take this one. He looks the most like Magnus and he might even make it as a show dog someday," Cal said.

Evander was surprised he'd choose one of the pups. "We do have the test results proving which are Dillon's and which puppies are Magnus's."

"No, I told you I trust you. You're a breeder like me and you know how important bloodlines are. I just want to look at the others to see how they turned out."

When Cal saw the other room full of Dillon's puppies, he smiled. "It's practically impossible to tell the difference."

"I know. They'll make good looking dogs no matter what."

"I agree. Okay, tell Alyth which one I want, and I'll be back in a couple of weeks to pick him up."

"Sounds good. In the meantime, he has a home full of puppies to play with all the time. He's having a ball."

Smiling, Cal shook his hand. "I know the feeling. Congratulations again on the two of you getting together."

"Thanks. Oh, whatever happened on Samuel Lemming's pups?"

"I had a vet verify they were Magnus's, especially since the dog napper had so many other dogs in his house. All twelve of Samuel's pups were Misty and Magnus's. But Samuel paid me a stud fee. I'm glad Samuel took possession of his dog before the dog napper ended up selling all those pups himself and that Samuel got his dam back."

"Yeah, same here."

Then they said their goodbyes and Evander let all the puppies out of the two rooms they had been in and into the main house again. Then he called Alyth. "Cal is getting Magnus, Junior."

"Oh, I told you he would!"

"You sure did. Well, how about steaks tonight to celebrate?"

"Absolutely. And champagne to go with it. Are you okay on your own for a while?"

"Yeah. We're good. Skye and the pups and I are going to settle down and watch a movie."

"Only cute stories, nothing too scary."

He laughed. "Only cute stories."

When she came home, she found him watching *101 Dalmations* with all the dogs. He was sitting on the floor, and she wanted to laugh. All the puppies were curled up all over him and Skye had her head on his lap. Alyth shook her head. "That's much too scary for the pups to watch."

He laughed. "They were so tired, they've been sleeping through most of the movie."

They had their steak dinner and Nita watched the dogs while they went on a wolf run at the MacNeill estate, then returned home. Nita had been getting in some wolf runs there too with others in the pack.

Alyth and Evander continued to move the pups outside for lots of playing, sitting down on the grass with them, and the dogs were all over them. They took tons of pictures of them and had them displayed in her shop, on Alyth's website, and social networking sites. Sometimes, they would have a couple of pups in the shop.

Everyone in the MacNeill Clan was sharing about them too. Talk about networking. The pups were quickly selling out, except for Nita's, Alyth and Evander's, and of course Cal's.

So that Nita's puppy, Magnolia, wouldn't be alone all day while Nita was working at the shop, they were going to have her stay with Skye and their puppy. And then Nita and Alyth would take turns playing with them outside, or when Evander came by for lunch, he would. Three of the people who had wanted pure-bred deerhounds in the beginning were just as pleased to pay less for the mixed breed, given that Dillon was the daddy, and both breeds of dog were so similar.

At eight weeks, they began to go home to their new families. "I'm beginning to feel like I'm having an empty-nest syndrome," Alyth said, though as the dogs grew bigger, they took up more room and were really underfoot. They had to make sure they didn't step on any of them. They were down to three extra pups now, plus Skye and Chiffon and Magnolia. But it was so much fewer with eleven of them having gone to their forever homes. All their new families were so eager to have them, most of whom had owned either Irish wolfhounds or Scottish deerhounds and loved their personalities. Alyth and Evander had made a chunk of extra cash for the shop, though it was doing great and so there were no worries there. The pack had paid the vet bills like they had promised. And Evander continued to keep the cottage so they could go there when they wanted to take the dogs for a run and run as wolves themselves. Even Nita used it on occasion for that purpose.

When Alyth returned to the house after a day at the shop, the last three of Magnus's pups had gone home with new families. She and Evander went outside with Skye, Chiffon, and Magnolia, and they all played in the yard.

Evander pulled Alyth into his arms and kissed her. "So what did *your* test results say?" That was the news he'd been waiting for all day.

She smiled up at him. "It's going to be a *very* long time before we're really going to feel the empty-nest syndrome. We're going to have a baby. Or two, who knows? We're wolves."

He lifted her off her feet and swung her around. "I couldn't be happier."

The pups and Skye chased around them, barking and excited about Evander and Alyth playing with each other, knowing it meant they wanted to play with them too. Tomorrow, the store was closed, and it was their day off, so it was time to celebrate.

But first, a call to the pack. They were adding some new pack members in a few months, and everyone would be thrilled.

After running to the grocery store, Nita showed up to pick up Magnolia and stay at the cottage to run as a wolf tonight with her pup and some of the wolf pack members, and Evander wondered if she was eyeing one of the bachelor males as a mate prospective. But she wouldn't say anything about it so all they could do was guess.

"We're pregnant," Alyth told Nita.

She shouted for joy, startling the dogs and gave Alyth a hug.

"I can't believe you and Evander are going to be having a baby, or two or three, soon. But I'm so thrilled."

"At least we won't be having as many as Skye's brood," Alyth said.

Nita laughed. "That would be way too much. I'm so happy for you."

"I'm going to have to hire someone to help out at the shop when it gets closer to my due date and after the babies are born."

"I'll help out all I can. That's the nice thing about working for a wolf pack," Evander said. "When it comes to wolf pups, the dads get lots of time off to help out with the kids. And believe me, a ton of wolves will want to assist with them too." Which was one reason he was so glad he was with a pack, for this eventuality alone.

Nita paused before she left and said, "Do...do the two of you want to have a night off together?"

They smiled and she took that as a yes.

Nita laughed. "Skye, Chiffon, come with your Aunty Nita. And yes, Magnolia, you're coming too."

They already had beds for them at the cottage and food, dishes, whatever they needed, plus the big yard to play in, so they were all set whether they stayed at the house behind the shop or at the cottage.

Evander and Alyth helped pack up the dogs and said good night to Nita. She said, "Don't worry about the dogs. I'll keep them for as long as you need me to tomorrow since we're all off from work." Then they hugged her good night and she left.

Evander took Alyth's hand and headed back inside. It seemed so empty in the house when the dogs weren't there, but no distractions either. "So what do you want to do for our unexpected night 'off'?"

"Dinner out? And dessert at home."

He smiled. "That sounds like our kind of night." They got dressed to go out and he took her to a seafood restaurant, but before they got out of the car, Alyth got a call.

"Ian," she told Evander, and he wondered what was wrong. She put it on speakerphone.

"Benji got a jail sentence of seventy-two weeks and a five-thousand dollar fine. We all feel it should have been more considering the pain and anguish all the families had gone through who had their dogs stolen by him, but at least he got some jail time and a fine."

"Maybe that will deter him from doing it again, but I doubt it," Alyth said.

"He'll have a criminal record this time, if he tries it again. If he does it in our area, and we learn about it, we'll give him a scare that will make him change his ways."

"Oh?" Alyth asked.

"He might just pick up the wrong breed of dog. One that's not exactly a dog."

Alyth smiled. "A wolf."

"Or two. And I'm sure we could convince him just how dangerous stealing dogs could be," Ian said. "I doubt he will try to steal Princess at Rebecca's house again either, after she clobbered him with a walking cane. I think someone like Benji needs other methods of persuasion. She hasn't had any other trouble since she returned home."

Evander rubbed Alyth's shoulder. He could tell she was much relieved. When it came to money, some people would go to any lengths to get it. Unless their life was in danger, perhaps.

"Well, Nita just arrived here to tell us she's serving dog-sitting duty for the two of you so you can share your special night celebrating being expectant parents. A bunch of us are going to run with her and let you enjoy your night," Ian said. "Oh, Julia says she is in charge of your baby shower."

"Thanks, Ian," Alyth said. "Thanks to all of you."

"Think nothing of it. That's what a pack is all about."

"Thanks," Evander said, then they finished the call.

They looked out at the fishing boats stranded at low tide on the water and saw the sky darkening with storm clouds. Evander took Alyth's hand and kissed it. "So if we have any trouble again with regard to anyone appearing to want to steal Skye, Chiffon, or Magnolia—"

"We show them that messing with our fur babies is bound to get terrifying. I can deal with that as a wolf."

"Yeah, me too." Then they went inside to get a table at the seafood restaurant and enjoy dinner and everything that came after.

But when they arrived home after having shrimp and lobster, they saw the front door was ajar. Evander parked the car and tore off his clothes. "Stay here for a minute." Then he shifted and ran into the house in his wolf coat, but Alyth soon followed as a wolf.

All they smelled was Nita's scent and she cried out, startled to see them. "Oh," she said, throwing her hand up against her chest, nearly dropping the bag of dog food under her other arm. "I called out, knocked, rang the doorbell, and I saw Evander's car was gone. I thought you were out enjoying yourselves. The cottage ran out of dog food and the store is closed. I didn't want to run over to the castle to get some in case they had a different brand of food there. So sorry. I'll be gone in a second."

Alyth ran past her into her bedroom, shifted, and came out wearing her robe. "No problem. Sorry we scared you. We were sure you were a dog thief."

"Ian told me what had happened with Benji and the sentence he got for dog napping, breaking and entering, etcetera."

"Yeah, and what we're going to do if anyone like him tries to steal Skye or the pups," Alyth said. She went outside with Nita while Evander joined them as a wolf. Alyth grabbed up their clothes. "That's why we shifted."

"I worry about the same thing also still. I'll do the same if anyone tries to grab Magnolia." Nita headed for the door. "Enjoy your night."

"Night, Nita," Alyth said, hugging her.

Evander woofed and then Nita drove off with the package of dog food. Evander had forgotten to buy some more for the cottage. Alyth shut and locked the front door. Evander shifted, pulled off Alyth's robe, and carried his naked mate to bed. "No more worries, at least for now."

"No, only a beautiful night in after a beautiful dinner out."

It started thundering and they smiled. He was ready to make love to his wife to finish celebrating the night. "Love you, Alyth. You are the joy of my existence."

"Love you back," Alyth said. "You are my dream hero who would swim a cold loch in the raw to rescue your dog and mine and give me the wickedest smile I'd ever seen."

He chuckled. "That loch was truly cold, but it was worth it to retrieve the two wayward dogs and meet the most delightful she-wolf I'd ever met in the world."

EPILOGUE

E vander showed up early at Alyth's shop after working with the dogs at the kennel, like he was known to do, worried about how Alyth was feeling. Months had passed since they'd learned she was pregnant, and she was due any day now. He kissed her. "How are you?"

"I think I feel like Skye did before she had her pups." Which was just the way Alyth would have her girl and boy—as a wolf, easier to birth. But not in their closet!

"Then that means you are due for a foot and back massage. If Nita can manage the shop alone?" Evander asked.

"Aye," Nita said, watching them, smiling and sighing. "If only Skye had been *mine* in the beginning, and I would have been so lucky to catch the Highlander."

Alyth laughed. "And then you would be in the shape I'm in." She rubbed her belly.

"At least you've been the perfect model for the new line of Highland maternity clothes, which has been so successful."

Alyth smiled. "I had to do something so I could still wear our merchandise. Not in a million years would I have thought I would be carrying maternity clothes on our online shopping service."

"All because of one runaway Skye," Nita said.

Evander headed Alyth out of the shop. "And one hot Irish wolfhound that had to make her acquaintance."

That had been the beginning of a beautiful relationship for two humans—who were a lot wolf too—a mating and now the start of their only family, not to mention raising one of Dillon and Skye's pups that had helped to prepare them so they would be ready for child/wolf pup rearing.

Evander and Alyth couldn't be happier and were now running as wolves along the MacNeill's beach nightly with Skye, Dillon, and Chiffon, the perfect outing for a wolf family and their dogs.

ACKNOWLEDGMENTS

Thanks so much to Donna Fournier and Darla Taylor for beta reading this book! And thanks to Lor Melvin who brainstormed with me—we definitely have twin brains—and helped me to come up with more of the story. All their comments were so helpful and much appreciated for this fun Highland wolf doggie tale!

ABOUT THE AUTHOR

Bestselling and award-winning author Terry Spear has written over sixty paranormal romance novels and four medieval Highland historical romances. Her first werewolf romance, *Heart of the Wolf*, was named a 2008 *Publishers Weekly*'s Best Book of the Year, and her subsequent titles have garnered high praise and hit the *USA Today* bestseller list. A retired officer of the U.S. Army Reserves, Terry lives in Spring, Texas, where she is working on her next wolf, jaguar, cougar, and bear shifter romances, continuing with her Highland medieval romances, and having fun with her young adult novels. When she's not writing, she's photographing everything that catches her eye, making teddy bears, and playing with her Havanese puppies and grandchildren. For more information, please visit www.terryspear.com, or follow her on Twitter, @TerrySpear. She is also on Facebook at http://www.facebook.com/terry.spear. And on Wordpress at: Terry Spear's Shifters http://terryspear.wordpress.com/

ALSO BY TERRY SPEAR

Adult Titles

Romantic Suspense: Deadly Fortunes, In the Dead of the Night, Relative Danger, Bound by Danger

***

The Highlanders Series: His Wild Highland Lass (novella), Vexing the Highlander (novella), Winning the Highlander's Heart, The Accidental Highland Hero, Highland Rake, Taming the Wild Highlander, The Highlander, Her Highland Hero, The Viking's Highland Lass, My Highlander

Other historical romances: Lady Caroline & the Egotistical Earl, A Ghost of a Chance at Love

***

Heart of the Wolf Series: Heart of the Wolf, Destiny of the Wolf, To Tempt the Wolf, Legend of the White Wolf, Seduced by the Wolf, Wolf Fever, Heart of the Highland Wolf, Dreaming of the Wolf, A SEAL in Wolf's Clothing, A Howl for a Highlander, A Highland Werewolf Wedding, A SEAL Wolf Christmas, Silence of the Wolf, Hero of a Highland Wolf, A Highland Wolf Christmas; SEAL Wolf Hunting; A Silver Wolf Christmas, SEAL Wolf in Too Deep, Alpha Wolf Need Not Apply, Between a Wolf and a Hard Place, SEAL Wolf Undercover, Dreaming of a White Wolf Christmas, Flight of the White Wolf, All's Fair in Love and Wolf, A Billionaire Wolf for Christmas, SEAL Wolf Surrender, Silver Town Wolf: Home for the Holidays, Night of the Billionaire Wolf, You Had Me at Wolf, Joy to the Wolves, The Wolf Wore Plaid, Jingle Bell Wolf, The Best of Both Wolves, While the Wolf's

Away, Christmas Wolf Surprise, Wolf Takes the Lead, Wolf on the Wild Side, Her Wolf for the Holidays, A Good Wolf is Hard to Find (2024), Dreaming of a Highland Wolf (2024), Mated for Christmas (2024)

SEAL Wolves: To Tempt the Wolf, A SEAL in Wolf's Clothing, A SEAL Wolf Christmas; SEAL Wolf Hunting, A SEAL Wolf in Too Deep, SEAL Wolf Undercover, SEAL Wolf Surrender

Silver Town Wolves: Destiny of the Wolf, Wolf Fever, Dreaming of the Wolf, Silence of the Wolf; A Silver Wolf Christmas, Between a Wolf and a Hard Place, Home for the Holidays, Jingle Bell Wolf

Wolff Family Lodge Wolves: You Had Me at Wolf, Wolf on the Wild Side, A Good Wolf is Hard to Find

Highland Wolves: Heart of the Highland Wolf, A Howl for a Highlander, A Highland Werewolf Wedding, Hero of a Highland Wolf, A Highland Wolf Christmas, The Wolf Wore Plaid, Her Wolf for the Holidays, Dreaming of a Highland Wolf

Billionaire Wolf Series: A Billionaire in Wolf's Clothing, A Billionaire Wolf for Christmas, Night of the Billionaire Wolf, Wolf Takes the Lead

White Wolf Series: Legend of the White Wolf, Dreaming of a White Wolf Christmas, Flight of the White Wolf, While the Wolf's Away, Mated for Christmas

Red Wolf Series: Seduced by the Wolf, Joy to the Wolves, The Best of Both Wolves, Christmas Wolf Surprise

Wolf Novellas: Day of the Wolf, Seal Wolf Pursuit, Wolf to the Rescue, Night of the Wolf, United Shifter Force

***

Heart of the Jaguar Series: Savage Hunger, Jaguar Fever, Jaguar Hunt, Jaguar Pride, A Very Jaguar Christmas, You Had Me at Jaguar, The Witch and the Jaguar, Dawn of the Jaguar

***

Heart of the Cougar Series: Cougar's Mate, Call of the Cougar, Taming the Wild Cougar, Covert Cougar Christmas, a novella, Double Cougar Trouble, Cougar Undercover, Cougar Magic, Cougar Halloween Mischief, Falling for the Cougar, Cougar Christmas Calamity, Catch the Cougar (Halloween Novella), You Had Me at Cougar, Saving the White Cougar, Big Cat Magic

***

White Bear Series: Loving the White Bear, Claiming the White Bear, Bear of a Halloween

Grizzly Bear Series: Bear in Mind

***

Wolves of Old: Wolf Pack

Vampire romances: Killing the Bloodlust, Deadly Liaisons, Huntress for Hire, Forbidden Love, Deadly Liaisons, Vampire Redemption, Primal Desire

Vampire Novellas: The Siren's Lure, Vampiric Calling, Seducing the Huntress

***

Comedy Romance: Exchanging Grooms, Marriage, Las Vegas Style

***

Science Fiction: Galaxy Warrior

Young Adult Titles

The World of Fae:

The Dark Fae

The Deadly Fae

The Winged Fae

The Ancient Fae

Dragon Fae

Hawk Fae

Phantom Fae

Golden Fae

Falcon Fae

Woodland Fae

Angel Fae

***

The World of Elf:

The Shadow Elf

The Darkland Elf

Warrior Elf

***

Blood Moon Series:

Kiss of the VampireMy Book

Bite of the Vampire

The Vampire Chronicles Series:

The Vampire in My Dreams

Demon Guardian Series:

The Trouble with Demons

Demon Trouble, Too

Demon Hunter

Non-Series for Now:

Ghostly Liaisons

The Beast Within

Courtly Masquerade

Deidre's Secret

The Magic of Inherian:

The Scepter of Salvation

The Mage of Monrovia

Emerald Isle of Mists

Made in the USA
Las Vegas, NV
06 April 2024